PRAISE
Glass Shatters

"*Glass Shatters* is a puzzle, one that both the reader and the book's narrator pick apart, deliberately circling a set of images, mere reflections, and shadows hinting at the truth, until reality comes devastatingly into focus. Meyers busts the detective story into pieces and digs through these shards to dissect memory, identity, and what it means to be alive."

—Brandi Wells, author of *This Boring Apocalypse*

"*Glass Shatters* is unlike any novel I've read before. It's an inventive, daring, and remarkable debut that pushes the edges of fiction with tremendous success. Michelle Meyers is certainly a writer to watch."

—Ivy Pochoda, author of *Visitation Street*

"Bold ideas explored with verve and imagination. Meyers is unafraid of taking the reader to bizarre and unexpected regions of this and other realities, along the way exploring the strangeness of existence."

—Charles Yu, author of *How to Live Safely in a Science Fictional Universe*

"*Glass Shatters* swept me up from the get-go. About a trail of lost and found memories in a world of genetic science, each sentence is as crystalline and vivid as recall can get. Tightly-plotted, it carefully walks and then fancifully deviates from the scientific through line, making both the novelist and science journalist in me applaud. Good work, Michelle Meyers!"

—Rebecca Coffey, author of *Hysterical: Anna Freud's Story*

"A puzzle and a page-turner, *Glass Shatters* invites readers into a dark investigation of one man's attempt to recover his memories and identity. Michelle Meyers has expertly crafted an engrossing novel with a sophisticated blend of art, science, and emotion, one that is ultimately an imaginative elegy on the arresting forces of love and loss."

—Gallagher Lawson, author of *The Paper Man*

"*Glass Shatters*, the truly uncanny, memorable novel of (among other things) memory presents itself as a transparent tale that soon (it does grow on you) transmutes into the translucent transcendental shades of Poe and Dick and James at his supernatural-est. This is domestic hyper-realism, turning ever irreal at the edges. The book is a magnificent machine, machining the senses and sensation. Michelle Meyers splinters feelings, running them through the ringer, a sieve so fine-tuned one begins to see the tinge and tint that spark, right there, off the spectrum, just out of insight."

—Michael Martone,
author of *Michael Martone* and *Winesburg, Indiana*

Glass Shatters

GLASS SHATTERS

A Novel

By
Michelle Meyers

SHE WRITES PRESS

Published 2016
Printed in the United States of America
ISBN: 978-1-63152-018-1 pbk
ISBN: 978-1-63152-019-8 ebk
Library of Congress Control Number: 2015954334

Book design by Stacey Aaronson
Cover illustration by James R. Eads

For information, address:
She Writes Press
1563 Solano Ave #546
Berkeley, CA 94707

She Writes Press is a division of SparkPoint Studio, LLC.

For my mother

Don't tell me the moon is shining;
show me the glint of light on broken glass.
—Anton Chekhov

PART I

I'm not sure if I'm awake. Colors, shapes, smells, and sounds meld together like an impressionist painting. Staticky voices ricochet through my head, the words indiscernible. I can't tell if the voices are my own or someone else's. Each heartbeat rattles inside of me as if I'm a machine that hasn't been used in a very long time. I know that something is irrevocably wrong. I know it the way people know their own mothers and fathers.

Rays of sunlight fight their way through the slits in the curtains and my pupils shrink to oily pinpricks. The living room gradually sinks into focus around me. I push myself up into a sitting position on the couch. A button on my back pocket snags, ripping a tear across the muslin fabric to reveal the yellow cheese foam underneath. Charlie Chaplin's *City Lights* plays on a small black-and-white television. Just as the Tramp and the Flower Girl touch hands on screen, their palms quivering against one another, a petal floats down from a vase of dead roses on the windowsill behind the TV. I blink once and then twice. There's a photo album sitting on the coffee table. I reach for the album and flip through the pages. Every single page is blank.

Then it floods over me, this realization, this fear, like a child who's lost and thinks he'll never be found. I don't remember anything about myself. I don't know my name, how old I am. I don't remember what I did yesterday, the last person I spoke to. I can recall the names of the things around me. And I remember that Woodrow Wilson was the president of the United States during World War I and that Watson and Crick discovered the double helix. But when I close my eyes, I see nothing, only a vast, empty void wrinkled by memories once had and now gone. The darkness is palpable, viscous black paint, and my thoughts are sticky, held in suspended animation. I open my eyes again and my attention is everywhere and nowhere at the same time. My tongue feels like a dry lump of clay in my mouth. I lap at the air, desperate to breathe. I will myself to relax, to allow my lungs to fully expand and contract. I'm going to be okay. Everything's going to be okay. I want to convince myself of this, even though I don't believe it.

A fat orange tabby cat struts across the living room, his tags jangling with each step like he's king of the place. He meows and bumps his head against my leg. I scratch behind his ears, try to keep my hands from shaking. He jumps into my lap, cooing for more. I check his nametag. Einstein. Not surprising given his wild mane of hair. I again breathe in deeply, counting to five before releasing it. All I can feel is sadness, a sadness that makes me wonder if I'm thirsty, and even that sadness is tepid, lukewarm. At least I think I'm in my own house. Einstein seems to enjoy my company, and while I don't remember anything, it all feels familiar somehow, the way the couch smells faintly like almonds, the slight springiness of the blue fiber rug.

There are no mirrors in sight. I look down at my hands.

They have fine blond hairs across the knuckles, well-trimmed nails. My limbs are long and lanky, and my feet look like ships in the brown socks I'm wearing. I'm male, white, most likely in my late twenties or early thirties. I touch my face. Slight stubble. Not wearing any glasses but probably supposed to be. I'm dressed in jeans and a gray plaid shirt that's tucked in. There's something on my head. I raise my fingers and find that it's a soft knit cap. My head throbs and I wonder if I was in an accident.

There's a pair of muddy footprints across the hardwood floor, leading to a pair of leather shoes by the couch that seem about my size. My gaze follows the footprints back to the entryway of the house. The front door is wide open and rattles with each gust of wind. I hear children screaming and playing, and with Einstein tucked in my arms, I approach the door. It's a brisk spring day, highlighted by sprays of bright pink rhododendrons in bloom, the sun occasionally peeking out from behind a thick layer of cumulus clouds threatening to rain. The maple trees are just starting to get their leaves back, and everyone's front lawns are crisp and green, standing at attention. I step down off the porch, watching a little girl with bright red hair tumbling in her yard a few doors down, doing somersault after somersault. A pattern of plump red strawberries stretches across her dress and she wears sparkly ruby-red slippers to match.

I look back at my house. It seems out of place in such a peaceful suburban neighborhood, a Gothic mansion like something out of Poe. Its peeling wood panels are covered with purple wisteria, its windows boarded up, the shutters hanging off their hinges. The paint is chipping. I can't even guess at its original color. The houses around it, in contrast, are friendly colonial revivals, modest and unassuming, painted rich reds and blues, perhaps to evoke American patriotism. They're the types of houses that have basketball hoops in the backyard and barbeques throughout the summer.

"Chaaarles!" a voice cries out from the distance, and the small bundle of the strawberry girl comes careening at me, her braided pigtails flying out behind her. She wraps her arms around my legs in a big bear hug. In my surprise, I drop Einstein, who scurries back into the house. At first I wonder if the girl will ever let go, but then she steps back, a strange look on her face, as if in her joy she'd forgotten she was angry with me. I reach out my hand, let it hang in midair between us, waiting, wanting to feel her warm, tiny hand against mine, the Tramp and the Flower Girl. She folds her arms against her chest, biting her bottom lip. I finally let my own arm drop.

"Where were you?" she asks.

I say nothing.

"You were gone for six months. You missed my birthday. I didn't think you were ever coming back."

"I'm sorry." I want so desperately to tell her that I don't remember. But I'm not sure it would be a good idea, so I don't.

"You could've said something. Before you left."

"I know."

"You hurt my feelings."

"I'm sorry. Truly." I mean it. I am sorry. I don't know why I would have left without telling.

"You hurt my mom's feelings too. She said you'd probably moved away. Did you forget about us?"

I wish I knew the girl's name. If I could just say her name. I look beyond her shoulder, out to the clouds sinking in a sky growing dimmer. I feel alone without my memories. I feel like a dinghy floating adrift.

"Why are you wearing a hat?" the girl says.

"What?"

"I've never seen you in a hat before. It looks weird. And are those bandages underneath?"

"Oh. I don't know."

"You look like you've been sick."

"Do I?"

"You're skinnier than before. And your skin is really white."

I kneel down so that the girl and I are face to face.

"Is there anything I can do to make things up to you? I really need you to be my friend right now."

"Promise never to leave again?"

"Okay. I won't leave."

I hold out my hand, and this time the little girl takes it, her handshake firm for a child her size. I realize I have no idea how old she is. Maybe five? Maybe eight?

I pause, willing myself to keep my voice steady, to not let it crack. "There's a game I'd like to play."

"A game? What kind of game?"

"Let's pretend I don't remember who I am."

"Why?"

"I don't know. Maybe I've been in an accident."

The little girl's eyes flash. "Or maybe there was an evil wizard who cut out part of your brain!"

"Yeah, let's go with that. That's much more interesting."

"And who am I?"

"Who do you want to be?"

"How about I'm a magic fairy who knows everything about you? And I find you wandering in the middle of the woods?"

Woods. Trees. Tall trees like redwoods, towering around me. I see flashes of gray, shadows, my own heaving breaths as I'm running away as fast as I can.

"Charles? Are you ready?" the little girl asks. I nod. The girl ducks out of sight for a moment and returns with a pair of leafy stalks that she tucks into the back of her dress as wings. She dances toward me, a ballet through the imagined woods around us, until she comes upon me, her small green eyes reflected in mine.

"You don't remember me?" she says.

I start to open my mouth, but then stop, simply shake my head no.

"I'm Ava, Ava Queen of the Fairies."

"Ava, what a beautiful name. And who am I?"

"You're Charles Lang," she says. She pretends to rub a magic ointment on my wounds.

"What year is it?"

"2012."

"And the date?"

"March. March something."

"And do you know how old I am?"

"Thirty-four. We had a birthday cake for your birthday in December even though you weren't here because I said we had to and my mom made sure there were thirty-four candles on the cake."

I take a breath, then: "And when I left, I didn't tell you why I was leaving?"

Ava frowns and acts as though she hasn't heard the question, picking red and yellow blanket flowers from the garden around the side of the house. "Would you like to eat some of these flowers?" she asks, approaching me. "They'll help you recover from what the evil wizard did."

I take the flowers and pretend-eat them. Ava looks pleased.

"How do we know each other, Ava Queen of the Fairies?"

"You're my neighbor and you're friends with my mom. You help her with stuff like fixing the roof and sometimes you let me play with your lab mice even though I'm not supposed to."

"Lab mice? Why do I have lab mice?"

"Because you're a famous scientist," she says, "like almost as famous as a movie star. Mommy says you make people new hearts and lungs and livers so that when they get sick, they can still stay alive."

"Ava?"

"Yeah?"

"Do you know why I feel so sad?"

Ava tilts her head down, stares at her feet. "Because you used to have a wife named Julie and a daughter named Jess but they disappeared one day and never came back."

"Ava!" a woman's voice calls out.

"I have to go, I have dance practice."

"Okay."

Ava hugs my legs again. "We were just playing a game, right? You remember who I am?"

"Of course, Ava. It was just a game."

"Good. Don't forget to feed Einstein. We were feeding him when you were gone but now you can do it."

"Okay."

I stand paralyzed as I watch Ava skip home, a fairy's bounce to her step. I close my eyes. A fragment of a memory—again I can see myself running through the woods, mud on my shoes, every breath lurching in and out like shards of glass pressing into my chest, distant flickering lights fading until I can't see anything anymore. I open my eyes. I wonder if this is all I have left. Why was I running? Was someone chasing me? Was I trying to escape from something? Or from somewhere? And why would I have disappeared six months ago without saying anything? I watch two boys playing catch across the street, listen to the *thwap* of the baseball each time it hits their gloves, and I wonder if maybe the memory loss wasn't the result of an accident after all.

"Wait!" I shout out after Ava. I don't want to be alone. Maybe her mother knows something more. I hop over a set of flowerbeds as fat raindrops begin to topple down from the sky. I run across the neighbor's front lawn. An old green Volvo station wagon rumbles in their driveway as Ava slides into the backseat, barefoot and carrying her ballet slippers. Just as Ava's mother is about to pull out, I jump behind the car, the Washington State license plate practically colliding with my knees. Ava's mother catches my eye in the rearview mirror. She slams on the brakes. Her mouth hangs open.

"Charles?" Ava's mother is out of the car now, a sweater over her head to block out the rain, both of us surrounded by the creeping smell of wet concrete. Her hair is curly and red with streaks of gray swirled in, and her pastel green eyes remind me of soap, clean and soft. She's dressed in pink nurse's scrubs that are slightly too long.

"I . . . I don't remember your name."

"Iris. It's Iris," she says with a controlled calm. Iris takes my hand as if she needs to feel the weight of it to confirm that I'm really there. Before I realize what I'm doing, I blurt everything out in a great tidal rush, about how I don't remember who I am, how I don't know where I was, how afraid I am. My eyesight blurs with tears as she gives me a hug, patting my back as a mother might for her son. She then lifts up my hat and examines the bandages underneath.

"It's going to be okay, Charles. We're going to figure this out. These bandages look clean, so my guess is that you were recently treated at a nearby hospital. I'll do some investigating at work today to see if I can pull up any records for you."

"Thank you. Thanks, really, I appreciate it."

"You know, in most cases, amnesia is a temporary condition. Your memory will likely return soon."

"Hopefully." My voice wavers. I'm not very convincing. "Iris, do you think there's any chance that someone may have injured me on purpose? I mean, what if it wasn't an accident? Should we call the police?"

"Usually when head trauma is caused by foul play, it's a lot messier. More bruising, more bleeding, fractures."

"Okay. All right." I breathe in deeply. "You're sure?"

Ava squirms in her seat, calling out for Iris.

"I'm sorry, Charles, I have to take Ava to dance and then start my shift . . . you can come with us if you don't want to be alone."

"It's fine. I'll be fine."

"Are you sure?"

"Yeah, yeah, I'll see you soon."

"I'll come check on you either tonight or tomorrow," Iris says as she slides back into the front seat. A moment later, the Volvo drives away, exhaust steaming through the cold air. I turn back around. My house looks more imposing than before, somehow reaching even further into the depths of the sky in the past few minutes. It's the type of house children would call haunted, that would have its own mythology. It's the type of house that would be reluctant to let go of its secrets.

I wipe the mud off my shoes on the fraying welcome mat. It says "Home Sweet Home" in curlicue letters. When I close the door behind me, I'm struck by how dark it is inside the entryway. It's as if someone has inhaled all the light in the room. I feel nauseated, my stomach turning, flipping over, and my vision gives way as if I'm walking through a fog late at night. Images flicker around me like old film spinning through a projector. A young girl in a ballerina outfit does pirouette after pirouette until finally she slips and falls, cracking her wrist against the floor. A woman in sweatpants reaches out to me, her glossy brown hair pulled back in a ponytail. She wipes away a smear of blood from a gash on her forehead with one hand as she reaches out to me with the other. She's never quite able to reach me. I close my eyes, sliding down against the wall. The woman and the girl eventually fade.

I stumble into the living room and lower myself onto the couch. They weren't real. It was just my imagination. Maybe Ava was lying. Maybe I never had a wife and a daughter. My brain feels sluggish, my feet like bricks. And I know, deep down, that what Ava said was true. I rest my head against a pillow and close my eyes, wanting everything to be the way it once was. I sleep a dense, dreamless sleep, yearning for a wife and daughter I don't remember, wanting to hold them against me, warm and happy and healthy.

I end up dreaming after all, of a small child curled up on a couch, his thumb in his mouth, his small glasses pressed up against his forehead. His blond hair is pushed up in sweaty tufts of sleep, and his cheeks are a warm pink. The television screen glows bright blue. The boy has his arm wrapped around a video game controller as if it were a stuffed animal.

The dream continues. The front door opens and closes. There's the slight crinkle of a coat being pulled off, the clack of business shoes against the hardwood floor. A tall man enters the room, sighing and loosening the tie around his neck. He spots the boy and nudges his shoulder. The boy opens his eyes and smiles.

"Dad—"

"Why aren't you in bed, Charles? It's past your bedtime."

The boy stands up on the couch. He's wearing pajamas with constellations on them, and he's missing one of his front teeth. "I beat it, Dad! All forty-two levels in Super Mario. There was this boss in the end who was super tough. Bobby and Andrew haven't even gotten past level thirty-five yet."

"That's enough, Charles."

"It's a really hard game, Dad."

"Charles—"

"I'm just saying, it was hard."

"Charles, video games are designed to be beaten. You haven't accomplished anything that tens of thousands of other children haven't already."

The boy frowns. The man gives him a pat on the head. "Go to bed, Charles. I'll see you in the morning."

When I open my eyes again, I can't tell whether it's nighttime or morning. I can't tell how long I've been sleeping. I can't shake the feeling that the house has something to hide. The dream with my father confuses me. Was it a memory? And why were we in this house? Why would I now be living in my childhood home?

I sink down to the living room rug, my legs sprawled out in front of me. I try to say my name so that it sounds real: "Charles Lang, Charles Lang, Charles La—"

With each attempt, though, the sound of the name dissipates in my mouth, the letters evaporating before I reach the end. The name doesn't feel like mine. I try again.

"My name is Charles Lang. I'm thirty-four years old. I'm a famous scientist. I had a wife named Julie and a daughter named Jess, but they disappeared one day and never came back."

As I say this last sentence, a chunk of white plaster falls loose from the ceiling, cracking against the coffee table. I watch as the bits of white powder gradually clear the air. I want to go home, to a home far away from here, to a living room where I can sit on a couch with Julie and Jess and watch cartoons and eat too much popcorn. I don't belong here.

My head feels like it's swelling, my scalp sweaty and irritated. I return to the entryway, hoping to find a mirror. No such luck. I know it's probably not a good idea to take off the bandages, but I can't help myself. The itching is unbearable. I search for a loose edge on the gauze and begin to peel the bandages away. They spread out in my hands like a snake's molted skin. The bandages are stained with eight small circles of brown blood, the circles oddly symmetrical. With each bandage I unravel, I feel an intense stinging pain. I bring my fingers up to one of the circles and feel the tender, oozing skin. It has the texture of a burn. But what would have created a pattern of burns like this? I replace the bandages around my head, worried that otherwise I'll get an infection.

I tilt my head back, close my eyes, and exhale a stale breath. I just want to find familiarity, to find out the truth. I open my eyes, and as they adjust to the light, I realize that I'm not alone. Instead, just above me in the rafters of the entryway are dozens of marionettes, beautiful young men and young women twisted around one another. I feel something shift in me, turning like cogs in a clock, as I descend into what I recognize could only be a memory.

August 1, 2004

Age Twenty-Six

A beautiful young man and a beautiful young woman sit in the living room, their limbs intertwined around one another. Their smiles are doused with light from the setting sun. The young man has brilliant blue eyes and thick sandy hair cropped close to his head. He wears a pair of tortoiseshell glasses, a white-collared shirt, and a pair of light-washed blue jeans that should've been thrown out last year. The woman has round hazel eyes and high cheekbones like apples. Dark hair pours over her shoulders. She wears a dress flowing down to her ankles and a necklace with heavy beads around her neck.

The young woman pecks the young man on the cheek and then stands, bending over the old leather trunk beside her and brushing the dust off the top. The latch has rusted over. The woman attempts to lift the latch. No luck. But then she puts her foot against the trunk and heaves backward, and the chest rattles open. The woman pulls out three wooden marionettes. They are simple, painted by hand—a woman, a man, and a child. Their hair and clothes are sewn from scraps of flannel, frayed pieces of denim, squares of cotton. The lack of uniformity in their outfits somehow makes them seem more alive.

"Do you remember? My mom used to tell us stories with these when we were kids," the woman says. She works at unknotting the marionettes' strings.

"Yes, I remember. But don't you think it's kind of disconcerting? I mean, the way they resemble us now?" the young man says.

"Oh, I don't know, I think that's just coincidence." The woman finishes with the strings and stands the male marionette and the female marionette next to one another. They look almost identical to the man and the woman. The child marionette lies immobile by the trunk.

"Now, let's see," the woman says, and she sits the male

marionette and the female marionette next to one another on the couch. She positions their small painted hands so that they're touching, just slightly. Their faces are turned toward one another and their posture is relaxed, casual and comfortable.

"May I?" the man asks. The woman pauses, then hands over the marionettes.

"My favorite story was the one that began on a rainy night in December," the man starts. "A man and a woman are curled next to each other, soaking wet, gazing up at the stars from the dry depths of a cave. They've admitted they love each other for the first time that night, even though they've known each other for years and years."

The man stops. He looks into the woman's eyes and plants a small kiss on her forehead. "And they're happy," he says, more quietly now. "They are happier than they've ever been."

I'M BACK IN THE ENTRYWAY, MY NECK CRINKLED BACK. I can't tell how long I've been in this alternate state. An hour? A day? But as I breathe out the claustrophobic air stuck inside of me, I can tell it's only been a few seconds, a minute at most. I take my face in my hands and rub at the heaviness that's still in my eyes. It was something like a memory. That's certainly the word I would use to describe the experience. And yet, if it was a memory, it didn't feel like my own. It didn't feel like something I lived but instead almost like a video recording. I could see the time and date imprinted, and it was as if I were an observer, watching someone else's home movies on a television screen. Except who else would the young man have been if not me? And who else would the woman have been if not Julie?

I look up above me, searching for the male and female marionettes from the story. They seem like they might be important, like maybe there's some sort of implicit knowledge stored in their wooden bodies. The marionettes are organized in rows of ten each, at least fifty altogether, their strings tied around the splintering rafters. I take a solid wooden chair from beside a bookshelf and balance myself on top of it, my head in among the marionettes. A layer of dust coats each one of them. The tips of my fingers are black within moments, my nose tickled, on the verge of a sneeze. I discover that the marionettes are, for the most part, different permutations of the same three figures—woman, man, and child—dressed up for different occasions, wearing different expressions. Some of the marionettes seem very happy—red grins are carved into their faces and their glass eyes gleam green and blue. Others are nearly destroyed. Pieces of their arms and legs have gone missing, their expressions scraped clear away. I move the chair back and forth among the rows, examining each of the marionettes. Eventually I realize that the ones I'm looking for, the male and female marionettes who confessed their love on a rainy night in December, no longer exist.

Back in the living room, Einstein greets me with a hair ball false alarm, hacking and coughing and then ultimately burping. I sit down on the couch and pick up a pen from the coffee table. I tear out a piece of paper from the blank photo album, writing in an unsure, chicken-scratch scrawl.

THINGS THAT APPEAR TO BE TRUE

1. *My name is Charles Lang.*
2. *I'm thirty-four years old.*
3. *I'm a famous scientist.*
4. *I have a wife named Julie and a daughter named Jess who have disappeared.*
5. *I'm living in my childhood home.*
6. *I disappeared from my house six months ago and this is the first time I've been back.*
7. *I'm friends with Iris and Ava down the street.*

QUESTIONS I HAVE

1. *How did I lose my memory?*
2. *Where did I disappear to six months ago? And why didn't I tell anybody?*
3. *What happened to Julie and Jess?*
4. *Are the memories I'm experiencing in fact my own? Or could they actually be somebody else's?*
5. *Why am I living in the house I grew up in? What happened to my parents?*

The walls creak around me as I write. I imagine that they're sympathizing with my frustration and exhaustion. I think for a moment, then add another question to the list:

6. *What has happened to all of the photographs?*

I don't know that I would've even noticed the absence of photographs if it weren't for all the empty frames scattered around the living room. All the paintings have been left behind, or at least the sorts of bland pastorals one might find in a doctor's waiting room. There are landscapes of beach sunsets and French villas in the countryside, watercolors of hot air balloons and white horses traipsing through Central Park. But there are no photographs, only tilted frames, cracked glass, and fingerprint smudges left behind as detritus in an otherwise clean house. Whatever was previously placed lovingly and thoughtfully into these frames has since been torn away and ripped apart in a hurry.

I stand up again and lurch forward, grabbing the arm of the couch. My skin feels dull and clammy, stars bursting across my field of vision. I smell pancakes, fresh blueberry pancakes sopping in yellow butter and maple syrup, and I see Julie again, perched by the windowsill in the kitchen, wiping her hands on a flowery apron, her shadow slowly seeping into the hardwood floor. The smell disappears. My stomach gurgles. I feel like I haven't eaten in days.

The door to the kitchen is cracked open and when I step inside, the first thing my eyes are drawn to is the cast iron stove, heavy against the wall. Initially I imagine that the stove is just an artifact, a relic of the past, but when I touch the surface, it's warm, recently used. Strange. The china in the cupboards looks like something out of the early twentieth century, handcrafted and chipped, the enamel worn beige in places. A faded daisy pattern winds around the rim of the ceiling. There's also a sleek metal refrigerator humming with electricity, though, and the hardwood floor looks like it's been refinished sometime in the past year. A series of cobwebs haunts the windowsill.

I open the refrigerator, expecting everything to be spoiled, the milk sour, the cheese moldy, a few cucumbers limp and rotting in their own juices. Instead, the refrigerator is fully stocked with fresh produce, lettuce and tomatoes and an enormous bunch of green grapes. There's a Tupperware of spaghetti sauce and another Tupperware filled with beef stew. I take out the carton of milk and give it a sniff. Nothing. I check the expiration date. It doesn't expire for another week. Meanwhile, Einstein stalks into the kitchen, his sleepy yellow eyes gazing up at me expectantly. He then turns around the edge of the counter and disappears, and when I follow him, I discover that he's gorging from a can of tuna. I nudge Einstein aside, much to his displeasure, and touch the tuna with the tip of my pinky. It's still wet. Has somebody has just opened it? For a moment I wonder if maybe Iris bought groceries for me, but that would make no sense. She hadn't known I was coming back.

I check the cupboards next, pulling them open one at a time. Every possible inch of shelf space is full, and I can't help thinking that this house would be well-prepared for an apocalypse. There are hundreds of cans of beans, soup, meats, and vegetables, their bright, bombastic labels perfectly aligned with one another. The cupboard adjacent to the stove is filled with plastic water tanks. A thought occurs to me. Before I left six months ago, when was the last time I'd left the house? Was I a recluse? Could I have been some sort of danger to myself?

Next I open the door to the freezer, curious and slightly frightened to see what else I might find, but the freezer is nearly empty except for a tray of ice cubes and a plate wrapped in tin foil. I unwrap the parcel, and it takes me a moment to realize what it is. But then I see the figurines on top, a little man in a tuxedo, a little woman in a wedding dress. This is a slice from my wedding cake. The ripples in the white icing are still perfectly preserved, a single pink flower swirling across the top. I hold the slice out in front of me, studying the spongy yellow cake, the buttercream icing, and most of all, the figurines, forever dancing together atop this slice of cake. This was me once. I was once the man in a tuxedo. I was once married to the woman in the wedding dress. I once ate a bite from this very same cake.

Suddenly I have an urge to throw the cake to the ground, to stomp on it, again and again, until the cake is nothing more than a few thick smears against the sole of my foot. If I could just remember what exactly Julie looked like, what exactly it felt like when she put her hand against my cheek . . . but instead, I have nothing more than a stupid slice of cake.

My stomach protests, acidic and foul, and I set the cake down to make a sandwich for myself. But even though the bread is fresh and the tomatoes are crisp and there's more than enough cheddar cheese, I can't take more than a couple bites before setting the sandwich down, tired and disheartened. Einstein leaps onto the countertop, nibbling on a slice of cheese that's hanging over the side of the bread. As I'm scratching him behind the ears, I hear something from the other room. Laughter. Deep, throaty, trundling laughs. Old timey music plays from the television, followed by more laughter. I scoop up Einstein with one hand and grab a steak knife with the other.

"Hello?" I call out, inching toward the doorframe.

The laughter continues.

"I have a knife. I could hurt you."

The laughter continues.

"I'm coming out, on the count of three."

Music and more laughter.

"One, two—"

I step into the living room, feeling a bit ridiculous, and find an old man sitting on the couch, slapping his hand against his knee as he watches a clip from *Casablanca.*

"Play it again, Sam!" he howls. He doesn't even notice me come into the room, his attention so focused on the television. I can't understand what's so funny. The man wears a dingy blue bathrobe, and his thin, clumping hair looks like the result of a chemical treatment gone wrong. His skin is purple, bruised and blotchy, his right forearm dense and creviced with scar tissue. A ratty scarf curls around his neck. Einstein jumps out of my arms and immediately hunkers into the old man's lap. I set down the knife and touch the man on the shoulder to get his attention. He turns, staring up at me, his big, blank eyes looking bewildered in spite of all the laughter. The old man doesn't seem fully alive, an echo of a human being.

"Hello?" I extend a hand, but he just continues to look at me, *through* me. Out of nowhere he starts to cry, tears streaming down his wrinkled face. I sit next to him on the couch and put an arm around his shoulders, feeling a warm wetness seep through my sleeve. The old man seems so familiar. I think of the principle of Occam's razor—the simplest answer is usually correct. There are millions of different people this man could be, of course, but the evidence only really supports one conclusion. Maybe it's odd that neither Iris nor Ava mentioned anything about me living with my father, but given his resemblance, his familiarity, I can't think of who else he could be. I begin to construct a narrative for myself, in which I'm living with him, caring for him as he experiences the advanced stages of dementia. I wonder how long my father has lived with me, how long he's been like this. I wonder who cared for my father while I was gone. I wonder what has happened to my mother.

"Are you—"

I realize that the old man has stopped crying and is now asleep, curled against my shoulder, his arm around Einstein. I slide out from under him and tuck him under a blanket, resting his head against a pillow. For a moment, his eyes blink open, and his face stretches and contorts. But then he closes his eyes again without saying anything, and within moments, he's fast asleep. I feel the couch beneath my fingers, the soft silky fabric against my touch.

August 9, 2009

Age Thirty-One

Little girls shove their airy bodies against the couch, straining themselves until the couch has been pushed to the side. They adjust their leotards and tights, turquoise leotards, fuchsia tights, sequins, wands, fairies swooping across the living room. The young man sits with the young woman on the floor. The woman's fingers squeeze those of the man. He rests his head on her shoulder.

"You looked tired," the young woman says.

"I can't sleep at night," the young man replies.

"It's gotten worse lately, hasn't it?"

The man shrugs. He looks like he hasn't slept in weeks.

The woman turns back to watching the girls. "Don't you love how children can dance without music?" she says. "And how they can have wild parties without needing a single other person?"

"I was never like that," the man says. "I could never do that."

The woman looks into the man's eyes, then takes his long-fingered hands in hers. They rise from the floor, and as the little girls leap and plunge around the room, the man and the woman waltz soundlessly around them. The man's footsteps are clumsy, awkward, but the woman is patient and graceful. When they stop, the man dips the woman down and then brings her back up, slowly, until her arms are around his neck.

"I love you, Julie," he says. "I love you so much that it almost hurts sometimes."

"But it's the best feeling, right?" she says. Her grin becomes menacing. Her arms tighten around the man's neck, until he is almost choking. "Isn't it a better feeling than anything else?"

I CAN TELL I'VE BEEN IN THE MEMORY LONGER THIS TIME. The old man has disappeared, and I can see through the curtains that it's now dark outside. For a few moments, whenever I close my eyes, I continue to see the little girls, swooping through the air in a way that defies gravity, to see the woman's malevolent grin, her teeth fading to nothingness. A shudder ripples down my back. I try to push the image away.

The memory still felt distant, as if I were watching something that belonged intimately to somebody else, and it's hard to imagine that I'm this young man. My stomach gnarls, my palms sweat, a chalkiness coats the inside of my mouth. I need to do something. I need answers. There must be a way to figure out what has happened to me, who I am, why I've lost my memory. I pull on a gray wool coat from by the door, stepping outside. I'll talk to Iris again. That's what I'll do. I'll go see what else she knows.

The air is surprisingly cold, stinging against my cheeks, and it isn't until I've walked halfway down the block that I realize I'm only wearing socks. I think about what I must look like, a shoeless, unshaven man prowling the street at night, and I catch a brief glimpse of myself in one of the windows. I'm shocked by how gaunt my cheeks are, like a skeleton just rising from the dead. My eyes are empty wishing wells, and my shirt is slack, hanging off my shoulders. I'm still Charles, still the same young man from the memories, but some sort of terrible transformation has occurred, leaving me a desiccated husk of my former self. I consider heading back but instead continue a few houses further down the block, careful to stay hidden in the shadows. And then I see them, Ava and Iris under the warm lights of the kitchen, eating dinner, talking and giggling. I'm surprised by how similar they look when sitting side by side, their cheeks blushing pink and then red with laughter. I can't help myself. For several minutes I just stand there, watching them, waiting, wishing that they would notice me. I want to knock on the door, to ask if I can join. I can't help but feel angry, resentful, jealous that I wasn't invited. I understand, though. We're friends but not family. Julie and Jess were my family, and now they're gone. Finally, Iris and Ava clear their dishes from the table, and I trudge home, pebbles jabbing into my feet, the woodsy smell of the nearby wilderness only making me feel lonelier than before.

I hang up my coat, then wander down the hallway, still wishing I had invited myself over for dinner. Suddenly I notice I'm standing in the middle of a room that feels like a dollhouse, a perfectly preserved and static world. A turquoise leotard sits atop the dresser, folded and pristine, the tags still on. There are wood block letters on the outside of the door painted with squiggles, polka dots, and black zebra stripes—JESS. For a moment I imagine movement in the room, but it's only the wind pushing a branch up against the window. The room itself is still, silent. The carpet is lavender with velvet curtains covering the windows, the edges uneven. The canopied bed is short and narrow, and the lacy white sheets are tucked neatly over the pillows. Posters of Russian ballet dancers are taped above the bed, holding difficult poses under bright stage lights. Along one wall sit dozens of porcelain dolls. Even knowing this was Jess's bedroom, I feel like the room has always belonged to the dolls. I sit down on the bed and take a worn fleece blanket from the end, wrapping it around my shoulders as I look around.

There's one doll in particular that strikes my interest,

wearing a lingering white wedding dress with puffed shoulder sleeves and jeweled embroidery along the bodice. The dark hair is pulled back to reveal black eyebrows and eyelashes painted with mascara. A veil drapes down her back, a bouquet of flowers clutched in her hand. I realize that the doll looks exactly like Jess.

August 4, 2010

Age Thirty-Two

The young man lies in Jess's bed, tossing and turning in the midst of a bad dream. He clutches Jess's teddy bear against his chest, wishing that his daughter would come back, just come back. His clothes are soaked through, his forehead covered with perspiration. He's in the throes of a nightmare. The chime of church bells strikes midnight. There's the looming presence of an altar, of an omnipotent God. An organist plays "Here Comes the Bride" but more of the pitches are off than on. The church's interior is obscured by darkness—all that lights the room is a single candle glowing from behind stained glass.

Jess walks down the aisle in her turquoise leotard and ballet slippers, wearing a veil torn at the edges and holding a bouquet of petrified flowers. Her skin is white as bone, her teeth yellow and decaying. Two large drops of blood have dried along her jaw, one just below each ear. Her hair is knotted with twigs and pine needles, and she's covered with bruises. She's five, maybe six years old at the most. A specter of a man stands beside her, a man that does not and could not ever exist, his arm around her shoulder, his hand squeezing tight. Jess squirms, trying to duck out from under him.

The lights rise to reveal the young man wearing a priest's robes. He thumbs through a Bible and begins reciting verses in a language that is at once incomprehensible. In fact, it is not a language at all, and what should be words are actually something less than sounds. Jess approaches the young man, pulling on his robes. The young man stops. He looks down at Jess.

"Daddy, why am I getting married?" Jess asks.

"Because you've grown into a beautiful young woman and that's what beautiful young women do," the man replies.

"But Daddy, I don't wanna get married now."

"Well why not, sweetie pie? If not now, then when?"

"I wanna run around the kindergarten yard. I wanna pet rollie pollie in a plastic bag. I wanna believe boys have cooties until they get their shots, and I can't become a famous ballerina if I'm married to him." She points at the specter, the invisible man. He tries to brush her hair out of her face. Jess flinches away. "Please, Daddy! When I'm older? When I'm grown up?"

"Oh, but don't you know? That's never going to happen, sweet pea. You're going to be five years old for the rest of your life."

"But—"

"It's a fact, my sweet darling. It's a fact, it's a fact, it's a fact . . ."

I'm in Jess's bed, my clothes icy with sweat. One of the scabs on the back of my head has bled all over the pillow, smelling brown and tinny. I turn the pillow over even though nobody will notice. *A nightmare. Just a nightmare, somebody else's nightmare,* I tell myself, breathing hard. I can't help dwelling on how small Jess looked, how desperate, existing somewhere in between life and death. Even if she is just a figment, a vestige of something dreamed long ago, I can't help but feel she deserves better than this, that she deserves family dinners and board games and strolls in the park. I can't help but be afraid that I've done something to cause this.

I get up from the bed, wiping away any last bits of the memory. I have to become methodical in my actions. Something tells me there's a logic to this house, a logic that should eventually become decipherable. I take a piece of paper out of my pocket, the one with the list of questions from earlier, and find a sparkly pink gel pen on the dresser. I draw on the back of the paper, a diagram of the rooms that I've already visited and the doors that I haven't opened yet.

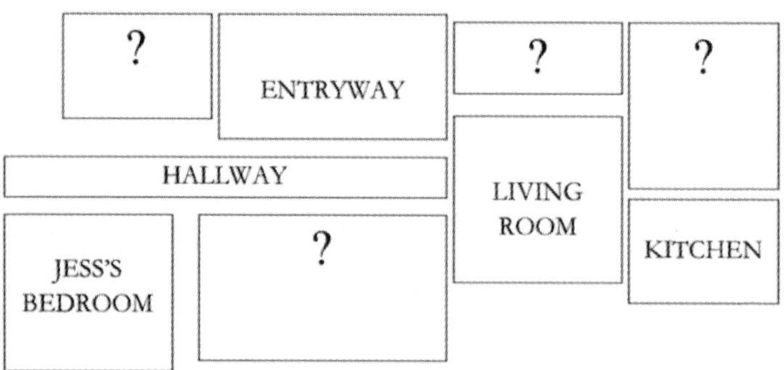

So there are four rooms left to investigate on the first floor, and of course, there's also a potential for an entire second floor. I say potential because thus far I haven't found any way to get up there, no stairs or ladder or anything like that. From the outside of the house, however, it's clear that there's at least one more story to explore.

I decide to start at the furthest end of the hallway and work my way back toward the living room and kitchen. The hardwood floor creaks with each step I take. I notice that the faint yellow walls are lined with empty picture frames. Some of them hang lopsided, as if someone rushed to remove the photographs. Others look like they've never been touched in the first place. I half expect the army of marionettes hanging by the front door to untie themselves from the rafters, to begin stalking me around the house. A part of me wonders if the old man is a ghost. I shake the thought out of my head. I'm a scientist. I can't believe in those sorts of things.

I turn the peeling lacquered knob to the door at the end of the hall. Nothing. I position my shoulder against the door and on the count of three, I heave my weight against it, turning the knob at the same time. The door groans open, and there's a rush of air, the room releasing a long held breath. The room feels like an artifact. I can't tell if it belongs to a ten-year-old child or a forty-year-old man. There's a queen-sized bed with a forest-green duvet folded over the sides, a vase of dried flowers once alive, a bookshelf featuring dense volumes on hydrozoans and cell mutation. But there are also baseball jerseys in the closet clearly sized for a young boy, an ant farm tipped over on one of the shelves, a Ouija board leaning against the books, worn copies of *Catch-22* and *Slaughterhouse-Five*. The wallpaper, a faded striped pattern that's also forest green, feels decades older than the springy gray carpet covering the floor. A pair of men's dress shoes sits next to a couple of scuffed sneakers, a framed Matisse print next to a Felix the Cat poster. I pick up the men's dress shoes, brown oxfords that lace up on top, and slide them on my feet. They fit perfectly. I feel a draft filter through the room and pull back the blinds to discover a broken window, right in the center, a circle with jagged edges about the size of a mouth. I wonder if it was just an accident, a neighborhood kid hitting a baseball too far. I suppose the hole is also the size of a fist.

A compartment in the headboard of the bed rests slightly open and I reach my hand in. There's a stack of old newspapers going back chronologically in time. I read over the headlines, the black ink rubbing off against my fingers.

"Can a Jellyfish Unlock the Secret to Immortality?
Charles Lang Thinks So"
(January 26, 2008)

"Charles Lang: How 3-D Printing Body Parts
Will Revolutionize Medicine"
(October 15, 2004)

"Charles Lang Awarded the Overton Prize in Biology"
(August 13, 2001)

I turn back further, back through the 1990s, the late 1980s. The papers are yellow and moth-eaten, and I'm concerned that they may just spontaneously disintegrate. I'm most shocked by the photographs of me, shaking hands with professors, pointing and gesturing at scientific charts and graphs. I'm grinning in all of them, absolutely beaming. I look happy and healthy, young and optimistic. I realize that Ava wasn't kidding when she said I was famous. I keep hoping to see Julie in one of the photographs with me, but there are none with her.

I finally stop at an article printed in September 1986. There's a large black-and-white photograph of a teacher in the center, a group of forlorn third-graders huddled on the auditorium stage behind her. One of the children is the small boy from my dream, Charles, the one who was curled up on the couch, waiting for his father. Of all the children, his face is the most absent, the most destroyed.

September 25, 1986

Age Eight

So I know that many of you may be wondering why we've gathered here today. Why are there so many people in suits with big cameras and microphones? Why are there big black vans in front of the school? Why did the mayor come by this morning to raise the American flag?" The teacher pauses to collect herself. She wears a black dress and black flats, her hair pulled back into a stiff bun. One of the students raises his hand, then slowly lowers it as he looks around the auditorium, realizing that the teacher was not expecting an answer to her questions. Reporters continue to bustle around the students as a middle-aged couple poses for photographs on the stage.

"The reason for all of this is that ten years ago today, a man came into the school and shot several children, and one of them died. His name was Gordy and he was in my third-grade class, just like all of you are. Gordy was very smart—he wanted to grow up to be a veterinarian—and he was also very kind. He was always sharing his lunch with other students, and he earned many merit badges in Cub Scouts. The man and woman standing on the stage are Gordy's parents, and even though they are very happy that we are all gathered here today to remember what a wonderful person Gordy was, it still makes them sad to think about him sometimes."

The small boy with the glasses raises his hand, squinting his eyes. The teacher hesitates but decides to call on him.

"Charles?"

"Why did he kill Gordy?" Charles asks without looking up.

"I don't know, Charles. Nobody does. It just happened. Gordy went to the bathroom to get a drink of water. The man who walked into the school was very angry and depressed. It could have been anyone."

"But he must have done something. He must have. He must," Charles insists, too quietly for the teacher to hear. For the rest of the day and the rest of the night, Charles doesn't say another word.

I'M STILL HOLDING THE NEWSPAPER IN MY HAND. THE article continues on page four. I turn to read the rest of the article, the columns blocking in a large photograph of Gordy, his second grade yearbook photo. He looks uncannily similar to Charles—the shock of blond hair, the round glasses, the missing front teeth—and I can see why Charles would have been disturbed. It's like looking into an alternate reality, a reality just as arbitrary and just as likely as the one that happened.

I squat down and examine the dusty bookshelf. There are books about Copernicus and Aristotle, Darwin and Newton, Einstein and Hawking. All of these suggest a young scientist in the making, someone who was determined to discover rules to the way the world works. I slip the newspaper article about Gordy into my back pocket, sure that if I were to leave it in the bedroom, it would somehow vanish. I don't trust permanence to be a rule in this house.

I then enter the room next to Jess's, on the side closest to the living room. The door is already slightly agape, and when I open it further and flip on the lights, I discover something completely different from the previous room. While both are sterile, appearing untouched for weeks or months, there was an asymmetry to the bedroom, to the way that it was laid out. In contrast, this room, which appears to be an office, supports an equilibrium, a balance to all of its disparate parts. Then again, how can there be asymmetry when the room is essentially blank? The walls are empty, a fresh coat of white. The bookshelves are empty, sterile metal. There are ten pens on top of the mahogany desk, five red pens on one side and five blue pens on the other, two fake leafy potted plants, each in opposite corners of the room. An expansive navy blue rug covers the floor. A small window hovers over the desk. There is no computer, no printer, no phone. There are no signs of modern technology.

I sit down in the desk chair, handsome black leather. I try to pull open one of the drawers but it won't budge. There's an iron lock on the left-hand side. I attempt the other drawers. The next two are both locked as well. When I try the top right-hand drawer, it slides open effortlessly, though, and inside I find a key next to a tin of paperclips and a roll of postage stamps. I take the key, sliding it into the iron lock. The first half of it manages to go in, but as I push further, the rest of it jams and then won't come out.

Maybe I should just leave this drawer alone. It's most likely nothing, office supplies, paper, or literally nothing, an empty drawer. But I want it to be the right key. Keys are supposed to fit into locks. That's what they do. I continue staring at the small, mangled key, willing it to transform into something useful. But then the desk catches my eye. It's slouching. The right side of the desk is notably lower, the wood warped and sagging. I lean down, placing my hand underneath the edge of the locked drawer, wondering if I can just pull it out, but I realize that I won't have to. The wood underneath is thin, worn through. I take off one of my shoes, pull my arm back and smash the thick leather sole against the bottom of the drawer, once, then again. The wood gives, and I smile at the destruction before me, the pile of splintered wood and debris. It feels good.

I dig through the fragments of wood and come upon a small oil painting, about four inches by six inches. The paint is peeling around the edges, revealing a yellowish canvas underneath. Two boys sit in the upper corner of the painting, so far away that they're barely discernable. One is tall and awkward, with rivers of blond hair spilling over his shoulders. The other is rounder with a head full of dark, curly hair. They sit by a lake, the sky swirling above them, as if it's about to rain. On the right side of the painting, a girl stands barefoot, gazing out at the viewer, only she doesn't have eyes, just empty sockets. There's something beautiful and delicate about her expression, yet haunting at the same time, and I just keep looking at the girl, imagining that she'll say something if I stare long enough.

May 11, 1994

Age Sixteen

"Charles! Dinner's ready!" Charles's mother calls out from the dining room. She enters carrying a large pot of spaghetti and a salad made with iceberg lettuce and blue cheese dressing. She wears a gingham dress with a frilled apron pulled around the front, beige high heels. Ringlets frame her round face and her eyes move back and forth across the room, taking in everything at the same time.

Charles's father sits at the end of a long oak table, tamping his pipe. His shirtsleeves are rolled up to just below his elbows, and the hair at his temples is beginning to gray. A Count Basie record plays in the background, and when the pin slips, Charles's father shakes his head, rising to flip the record to the other side. A bookshelf filled with leather-bound classics stands against one wall, The Iliad *and* Moby Dick *and* A Tale of Two Cities. *On the adjacent wall is a painting of the family sitting in a studio with emerald-green drapes hanging behind them. In the painting, the father's expression is stern. The mother purses her lips together, holding a baby bundled in her arms.*

Charles trips into the dining room, his limbs awkwardly long and gangly. He wears a sweatshirt and sneakers, a pair of bulky headphones around his neck. He's older now and although he's not nearly as tall as his father, he's no longer a child either. His hair has darkened slightly and comes down past his shoulders. The edges of his jaw are covered with acne. And yet he has become handsome, in an academic sort of way. He pushes his glasses up with one hand as he holds his place in a scientific textbook with the other. His nose remains in his book as he sits down.

"Charles, not at the table," his mother says, and Charles places the textbook under his seat. "Thanks, sweetheart."

Charles's mother and father sit at one end of the table, Charles at the other. As they pass the spaghetti, Charles's father takes a final puff from his pipe, then sets it down. Charles's mother squeezes her husband's shoulder. His eyes are milky blue, clouded and glossed over, and his right hand shakes as he brings a bite of spaghetti to his mouth. The spaghetti noodles topple off the fork and into his lap. Charles's mother discreetly wipes them away and plants a kiss on her husband's cheek.

"You know, I read in the news today that South Africa just swore in their first black president. Nelson Mandela. Isn't that something?" Charles' mother tries. His father shrugs and picks at his teeth.

"Well, how was work then?" she asks.

"It was all right. You know, work."

"Any new studies?"

"I spent the day washing all of the lab equipment. The beakers are very clean now. Very, very clean."

"It can only get better, right?"

Charles' father turns stiffly to his wife. "How was your day, darling?"

"Hectic. Went to the market. Ran errands. Oh! And as I was walking home, I bumped into Julie's mother."

"I don't know who Julie's mother is."

"Yes you do. Mrs. Hollingberry. Today she was standing barefoot in the front yard, wearing an African robe and 'reading' her wind chimes. She invited me in for a cup of gingko nut tea and when I tried to say no, she insisted on giving me a pouch of herbs to heal the incongruities in my aura. Last week she offered to do my astrological chart, and the week before she roped me into a tarot reading only to warn me of my 'impending doom.' There are puppets and marionettes scattered all around the house. I can only imagine what she keeps behind closed doors."

"Right."

Charles's father takes a large bite of salad. Charles's mother continues. "It really is too bad. I mean, poor Julie. She must be so embarrassed. At the school play last fall, Mrs. Hollingberry was sobbing by the end of it, and you could hear her throughout the entire auditorium."

"No father?"

"No, just the two of them."

Charles's father looks up from his food. "How does she support the child without a husband?"

"I heard that a few years ago she published a very popular book on the occult, and I imagine there must be some sort of inheritance as well. Plus, from the looks of her house, they live on nothing."

"Mom, can you pass the spaghetti?" Charles asks. There's an edge

to his voice. His mother hands him the pot without seeming to notice.

"Charles, you've been spending a lot of time with Julie lately. You should invite her over for dinner. I don't imagine Mrs. Hollingberry devotes much time to grocery shopping or other more practical matters."

Charles's father looks up from his plate and gives Charles a strange smile. "Aren't you glad your father is a scientist and not some sort of spiritual quack? Let me see that book you were reading." He reaches across the table. "What are you studying up on? Electromagnetism? Stoichiometry?"

"Nah, it's okay. No books at the table, right?" Charles says, pulling the book away.

"Come on, Charles, show me the book."

"I said no."

"What, you think I won't understand it?" Charles's father slams his fork against his plate. "You think you're smarter than I am just because—"

Charles stands up. "Mom, I'm not hungry anymore—may I be excused?"

"Charles, you answer me when I speak to you!"

Just then the doorbell rings. "Why don't you go see who that is?" his mother says. Charles picks up the textbook and takes it with him. He hears his father from behind him, stuttering, his voice catching, the snuffling of Charles's mother in tears.

When Charles reaches the front door, he peers through the peep-hole and then draws back. He runs his fingers through his hair to smooth it out.

"Charles, is that you?" calls out a young woman's voice.

"Yeah, one sec!" Charles says, trying to smooth out his hair more vigorously now. It's impossible.

"Whatcha waiting for?" the voice calls out, and Charles opens the door. They stand for a moment, neither saying anything. The girl is Julie, around fifteen years old, wearing a purple paisley dress and hemp sandals that wrap around her ankles. Her hair is short and springy, a daisy tucked behind her left ear. She carries a knapsack filled with carrots and art supplies, and her perfume smells faintly like almonds.

"Want one?" she asks, handing Charles a carrot. "They're fresh from the garden."

"Yeah, sure," Charles says. Charles puts it in his pocket with the green stem sticking out. "I'll, uh, I'll save it for later."

"So did you finish it? What did you think of the end?" Julie asks. Charles opens the textbook and pulls out a comic book from the middle.

"Cause of your dad?" Julie says.

"Yeah, he'd think it was a waste of time. Or at least, he would've. Now that he's crazy and all doped up, I don't know what he thinks," Charles says. He hands the comic book back to Julie.

Julie nods. "What did you think?"

"It was really great. I, uh, I loved the illustrations."

"And the story? Isn't Raven a fucking badass?"

"Yeah, she was pretty awesome."

"But?"

"But what?"

"You've got that look on your face. You hated it, didn't you?"

"No, of course not. I didn't hate it, it's just . . . you know, it was pretty implausible. I mean, it had a lot of great moments, but, I don't know, I didn't really buy the ending. It didn't really make sense."

"That's the point of comics—you can do whatever you want! Who cares if the likelihood of getting bitten by a cybernetic spider is a million to one or if you can't, like, teleport or shoot laser beams in real life?"

"I guess I care." Charles looks down at his feet. "I'm sorry."

"Duh, you don't have to apologize, Charles," Julie says, sliding the comic book into her knapsack by the carrots.

"I want to like it."

"I know you do. We'll find something you like—you know how many comic books and fantasy novels I own?"

"A lot," Charles says, smiling.

"You'll like one of them. I can guarantee it." Julie reaches for Charles's shoulder and gives it a squeeze.

"I was planning to meet Steve at the reservoir," Charles says. "You wanna come?"

"Yeah, sure thing. I just need to go home to grab a sweater."

"You can take mine. I'm never cold." Charles peels off a purple sweatshirt with the University of Washington logo and hands it to Julie. They walk in silence, weaving through backyards until they find the dirt path that leads down to the reservoir.

"So how is your dad doing?" Julie finally asks. The sun is starting to set, but they've been down to the reservoir so many times that they have no trouble finding their way.

"I don't know, better? He's back at work, so that's good, and he's not having delusions or hallucinations anymore, or at least not that he's telling us. But the clozapine also makes him kind of like a zombie, except for when he's angry. Then his temper's way worse than it used to be . . . Oh, and I have news—my mom's having an affair. She thinks I don't know but I do."

"Yikes. Your parents remind me of a repressed 50s couple gone horribly wrong."

"Right? It's like they're out of another era. Sometimes I just want to stuff them back into a black-and-white TV set where they belong."

They're getting nearer to the reservoir. The air has an earthy smell to it. "Well, if it makes you feel any better," Julie says, tucking her hair back behind her ears, "my mom told me yesterday that I was an accident. I mean, whatever, accidents happen, right? But you know what the worst part is? She said she wishes I wasn't born because some voodoo witch doctor something or other said that if my mom did have a child, the child would die young in a horrible accident. Ergo, every time I go outside, she's convinced a plane is going to fall on me or an earthquake is going to hit."

"Ouch. Well, you better not tell her about all the heroin you're doing or all the knife fights you've been getting into."

Julie shoves Charles in a playful way. "Haha, very funny. I'm surprised she lets me out of the house without a full suit of armor and an EpiPen."

"You two think your parents are bad?" a voice chimes in behind them. "Try being gay in a household of evangelical Christians. I woke up last night to my mother standing over me with a feather duster. She was trying to give me an exorcism. I swear, next time I wake up in the night, she's gonna come at me with a butcher knife, speaking of knife fights."

"Hey Steve," Charles says. He gives Steve a big pat on the back. Steve is short and stocky, his skin smooth and cherubic compared to Charles's pockmarked face, a hedge of curly black hair on his head.

The group reaches the reservoir, and as Steve and Charles sit down by the water, the scene looks almost exactly like it did in the oil painting. The thunderclouds above are thick like sludge, but still Julie slides off her sandals, burying her toes in the dirt. She pulls her sketchbook and a charcoal pencil from her knapsack and begins drawing.

"You know, we don't have to settle." Julie continues to sketch, shading in one of the figures. "We could run away together. We could start our own family, just the three of us."

The last of the sun drips down below the horizon, and they lay back under the twilight blue sky. Charles's shoulder presses up against Julie's. He knows he could shift away but leaves his shoulder against hers.

Charles closes his eyes. He imagines what life would be like if they ran away together. He imagines living in a small cabin in the forest, away from civilization, chopping their own wood, growing their own food. Most of all, he imagines waking up every day to see Julie sleeping beside him, and at that moment, he realizes this is something he'd very much like to happen.

By the time they get up, it's already dark out, and Charles can't get enough of Julie's face in the moonlight.

I TURN THE PAINTING OVER. HER SIGNATURE SWIRLS across the canvas in a stream of black ink: *Julie H., 1994.* I trace the letters with my index finger, wondering why Julie wasn't sitting with Charles and Steve in the painting, wondering where her eyes have gone. I think of the memory with the marionettes, of the rainy night in December. When did we finally admit our love for each other? How did I feel when she said she loved me back? I set the painting on the windowsill, hiding it behind the curtains, hoping that it will be there when I return. I close my eyes, giving in to an enormous yawn, the painting warping in my mind, Julie cowering beneath my open hand, her empty eye sockets elongating into screams. I shake the image out of my head. What if Julie and Jess didn't disappear but left? What if they were running away from me?

I tell myself not to think about this anymore. It's too late. I'm too tired. I plod back down the hallway, slipping off my shoes at the entrance to what I've now come to think of as my bedroom. Through the window, I can see the sky has become almost orange, like the flesh of a peach. I've stayed up nearly all night long. But the room is still dark, and the rising sun casts gaping shadows across the bookshelves and the wall.

I climb into bed without even taking off my clothes, the exhaustion like a lead apron, weighing me down. I slide under the quilts and sheets, but as I dig my feet under the warmth, the bed is even warmer than I anticipated. My left hand comes across the old man's shuttering chest, rising and falling with each breath, so frail that each rib is completely distinguishable from the next. I curl up next to him, resting my head against his shoulder, the peaks and valleys of whatever relationship we may have had irrelevant in this single moment. I imagine I'm a little kid again, and this time, I get along with my father.

With a jingle and a thump, Einstein jumps onto the foot of the bed. He makes his way up to the pillows and wedges himself between the two of us, letting out a satisfied lawn-mower purr as he settles into a more comfortable position that of course takes up the majority of my pillow. Our heartbeats all fall in sync together.

For the first time since I've been in this house, I feel safe. I feel at home.

~

I WAKE UP THE NEXT DAY ALONE IN THE BED. THE pillows are covered with a layer of cat hair. When I stretch across to the other side of the bed, I'm surprised by how cold the sheets are. I think about what it must feel like to lose a spouse suddenly. I wonder what that first morning without Julie felt like for me, losing that warmth, that love. I get up and peer through the window—the children outside squeal and laugh as they splash through the puddles, mud soaking through white T-shirts, parents in rain boots squashing around after them, teeth chattering in the blustering wind.

I then hear a loud, oaky knock, followed by the echoing chimes of the doorbell. I take a peek through the broken window and see Ava standing on the steps. She has on rainbow galoshes and a ladybug umbrella, and her hair is pulled back in pigtails. She holds a basket of homemade chocolate chip cookies in the crook of her arm, ringing the doorbell again and again. I smooth down my shirt, trying to push away the wrinkles. I touch my short hair. It's standing straight on end. My lips are dry and cracked like sunbaked clay. I need to wash up.

Ava looks me up and down when I answer the door. She hands me the cookies with the very tips of her fingers, attempting to keep the greatest distance between her and me.

"You really don't want to get close to me, do you? How awful do I look? Hopefully I don't smell that bad."

"Your head," she says, staring at my scalp as if it's covered with flesh-eating insects. I realize that the bandages must have slipped off while I was asleep.

"What does it look like?"

"What happened to you? Are you dying?"

"I don't remember what happened, but I'm not dying. One sec," I say, and I pull the knit hat off the front rack, sliding it over my ears. I had never even thought of that possibility, that I have some sort of chronic illness, that maybe I've had surgery for cancer, a brain tumor. But if that were the case, I wouldn't have been left alone with my father. Unless I sneaked out from the hospital? No, probably not. I slow down, tell myself again that the simplest answer is most likely the correct one.

I turn to Ava, striking a pose, modeling the hat for her. "Is that better?"

"Yeah, sort of. How come you're wearing the same clothes as yesterday?"

"Because I thought I just looked so good in them."

"I don't think that's true," Ava says. She takes a cookie from the basket and chews on the edge. "Do you want to come over for dinner tonight at six? My mom said to invite you over cause you'll probably be sad all by yourself . . . oh. I wasn't supposed to say that part."

"It's okay, I appreciate it. Six sounds good."

"Make sure to shower and put on new clothes and a hat cause my mom would be afraid of your head too. It's already five so you should do it soon."

Right at that moment, the old man passes behind me in his dark robe and slippers, cradling Einstein in his arms like a baby. He pauses, studying Ava like a laboratory specimen, his lower lip drooping open. Then he wipes his nose and disappears into the living room. I hear the television flip on.

"Who's that?"

I lean down so that I'm at Ava's level. "That's my father, Ava. He lives with me now. He's very old and sick, so sometimes he does strange things."

At first, Ava doesn't seem to register what I said, but a moment later, her cheeks flush red.

"I have to go," she says, dropping the rest of her cookie and running out into the rain. Lightning streaks across the sky, a drumroll of thunder crashing in the distance.

"Ava, wait! What's wrong?" I call after her. She doesn't turn around. Her rainbow galoshes splatter through the mud. Her ladybug umbrella lays sprawled on my front porch. I gather the basket of cookies and the umbrella, ducking back inside. I wonder what set her off like that. I didn't say anything provocative or out of the ordinary. Maybe it was just a delayed reaction to the old man? Or maybe she just noticed the marionettes for the first time. I imagine how frightening it would be, seeing all of those ghoulish faces staring back at you.

The only door on the first floor that I haven't explored (either in real life or in a memory, as in the case of the dining room) is the door at the front of the living room by the entryway. The knob turns easily and it is indeed a bathroom, the walls inside royal blue, the paint bright—a recent coat. There's a toilet, a shower, a sink, and several hand towels. I turn on the faucet and take a few large gulps of water from my cupped hand. I can't get enough. I stick my mouth under the stream to drink even more. When I finally lift up my head, wiping the water from my lips, I notice a seam running down the wall, ending just above the sink. At the very bottom of the seam, a corner of the wallpaper is starting to peel up, just a fraction of an inch. I take the corner in my hand and pull. The dense layer of paint over the seam begins to crack. I can't help myself. As I continue pulling, more of the wallpaper starts to come off. The section above the sink must have been a later addition.

With one last yank, the entire section of wallpaper peels off, leaving behind a gluey residue. I turn the faucet to hot and take one of the hand towels, soaking it with water and soap. I scrub vigorously at the glue, put my whole body behind it. My suspicions are confirmed as more residue rubs away. The extra piece of wallpaper was plastered over a mirrored cabinet. I hold my breath as the first small circle of glass appears underneath. I work at the edges. The circle widens.

It's the first time I've seen myself up close. I recognize the solid blue eyes gazing back at me, the blond hair cropped close to my head. Every detail of my features looks like those of the Charles from my memories, memories that I'm now sure have to be my own. Except that I'm thinner now, thinner than I should be, my eyes leaner and emptier somehow. But there's still warmth in each smile I try, with teeth or without, broad or slight.

I scrub at the glue residue at the edges of the mirror, and with a firm tug, I'm able to pull open the cabinet. There's an assortment of bathroom products, lotions and razors, cologne and old toothbrushes. Tucked away on one of the shelves is a tiny square picture frame, the back facing outward. I expect it to be empty, abandoned like the others, but it holds a photograph of Julie in a royal blue dress.

March 1, 1996

Age Eighteen

Charles approaches the art room as one might approach a military reconnaissance operation, with equal parts caution, trepidation, and excitement. The school yard looks like foreign terrain in the moonlight, and Charles goes through a circuitous routine of loosening his tie, licking his lips, and checking to make sure that the flowers in the bouquet are still fresh. His hand quivers on the doorknob. It sounds like a hive of bees inside. His tie is so loose now that it's hanging in a wide loop around his neck.

He expected a small gathering for the senior exhibition, a handful of art students and their parents, a single bottle of grape juice, and some stale crackers from last year. Instead, the school has transformed the art room into a gallery capable of competing with the very best of Los Angeles and New York. The students have cleared away the clutter, the benches and tables and art supplies. The walls are the clean, blank-slate white of museums, and caterers weave back and forth through the crowd with hors d'oeuvres and sparkling apple cider. Reporters from the local paper snap photographs of artists and their work. One of the artists walks by with an entire armful of roses. Charles looks down at his lilies and tries to spruce them up a bit.

"Hey Charles, over here!" a voice calls out, and Charles looks over to see Steve's curly hair bobbing up and down in the crowd. Charles makes his way to Steve, trying not to get elbowed in the process. Steve is wearing a full tuxedo with a ruffled pink shirt and a matching bow tie. Charles feels a bit sheepish in his jeans and brown corduroy jacket, but then again, it's not like he owns any clothes fancier than that.

"This place is a madhouse," Charles says. "I didn't realize this was such a big deal."

"Dude, our high school has the top-rated art program in all of Washington. This is the future generation right here."

"Where's Julie?"

"They're still setting up her installation in the back—she should be ready in about five minutes." Steve eyes the flowers in Charles's hand. "So you gonna ask her?"

"Ask her what?"

"Are you going to ask Julie to prom tonight?"

Charles swallows, a baseball-sized lump in his throat. His cheeks grow warm. "What are you talking about? I thought we were going as a group."

"Don't be an idiot. You have to ask her out."

"Steve—"

Steve takes Charles by the shoulders. "Charles, listen to me. Julie is the most beautiful girl at this school, both inside and out, right? So why hasn't she had a boyfriend yet? Because she's been waiting for you. And if you keep waiting, someone else is going to ask her out, and she's going to say yes."

Charles looks down at his lilies. He's afraid he's going to squeeze the life right out of them. "But what if she doesn't like me in that way? What if I ruin the friendship?"

Steve pops a stuffed olive into his mouth, downing it with a plastic cup of cider. "Trust me, Charles. You have to trust me on this."

"Has she said anything to you?"

Steve ignores Charles's question and points. "Come on, I haven't seen the piece in that corner yet."

Steve stops in front of a video installation, black-and-white footage of a man in pajamas sitting in a small cement cubicle. After a few seconds, the man begins screaming, pulling off his clothes, and throwing himself against the wall. Several orderlies rush in, trying to sedate him. The camera zooms in on his bulging eyes, his salivating mouth. Charles reads the plaque beside the streaming video: "Schizophrenia Untouched." He can feel his chest tighten. He ducks under several people's arms, determined to escape the horde, to get out. He plunges through the door and sinks down against the brick wall outside. Steve follows after him.

"Hey, hey, that's it. You're okay. Just breathe."

Charles feels the cold night air in his lungs. He closes his eyes. He pictures Julie. He pictures Julie smiling at him. His breaths slow down.

Steve sits next to Charles, his legs sticking out in front of him, his tuxedo pants getting dirty from the gravel and dust. "You know, I had a great uncle who was schizophrenic. He was diagnosed in the early 1950s and was locked up in mental hospitals for over ten years. Finally they got him on Thorazine and the hallucinations and delusions stopped. And he was more or less himself again. Except that he never forgot those years being locked up. It destroyed him."

"Yeah? So what if that's me, Steve? What if that's me in ten or twenty years? It has a genetic component, you know."

"It's not going to be you, Charles. You're not your father."

"And if, you know, if I do . . ."

"Look, I'm always here for you. What I was trying to say earlier is that I would never let anybody send you away and lock you up. I know better than to let that happen. I promise, okay?"

Steve extends a hand to Charles. Charles hesitates, then takes Steve's hand in his, returning his gesture with a firm shake. He notices that the stars above have stopped spinning. He stands up, brushing off his jeans.

"C'mon, let's go see Julie's exhibit," Steve says. He acts as a buffer for Charles against the crowd, nudging people out of the way and creating a clear path. A group has gathered in the back, presumably around Julie's installation. Steve pushes their way to the front. Charles looks down. He was sure he'd dropped the lilies but no, he's held onto them, and as he sees Julie, he grins at the fact that they will go perfectly with her dress, a deep blue dress as rich as the sky at twilight. Her hair is done up, whirling above her head, and a single string of pearls lies against her collarbone. She curls through the crowd, creating a riptide, as people swell back toward her, eager for handshakes and discussions of aesthetics.

"Look," Steve whispers, gesturing toward the walls around them, and Charles turns away from Julie. The walls are covered with photographs, candid photographs of Charles, at the lake, in the woods, at school, at his house. In some, the lens is so zoomed in that he can see the very pores in his skin. In others, he's merely a

speck in the distance. There is nothing idealized about these photographs—in all of them, Charles is honest. Charles is himself.

Charles reads the placard beside the exhibit:

Portraits of a Real Boy

Julie Hollingberry, 1996, Oil on Canvas

These paintings draw inspiration from the earlier photo-realists such as Robert Bechtle and Chuck Close, and for many, they will seem indistinguishable from photographs. I seek to demonstrate the transcendent beauty of representational veri-similitude to the highest degree. Rather than requiring one to veer into the realm of abstraction and fantasy to discover truth, I hope to show that mimetic art, art that acknowledges the banalities, the grittiness of everyday life, is capable of the great-est emotional resonance and psychological realism.

Charles feels a tap on his shoulder and turns to discover Julie behind him, in all of her magnificent splendor. He has never seen her with her hair up before, and it only serves to accentuate the outline of her cheekbones. He hands Julie the lilies. She blushes as she takes them.

"I'm glad you came tonight, Charles." Julie plants a small peck on his cheek.

"I'm glad I came too," Charles says. His face feels so warm, especially in the spot of the kiss, he is sure he is about to spontaneously combust.

I knock lightly on the door to Iris and Ava's house, a white door with a stained-glass window. The rain has stopped but thunderclouds still swirl overhead. Their mailbox is full and one of the letters has floated down to the ground. I pick up the damp envelope and read the address:

Iris Brenner
157 Maple Rd.
Hillston, WA 98409

Iris Brenner. Maple Road. Washington. The words roll off my tongue as I say them to myself. I hope I've cleaned up well enough. I took a shower—the water so hot it practically singed my skin—shaved the stubble, cleaned under my fingernails. I'm wearing a light blue dress shirt, gray slacks, a navy blazer, and a black trilby hat I found in the back of the bedroom closet. I check my jacket pocket, making sure that the photograph of Julie is still tucked in there. I couldn't leave it behind. She's so real in the memories, I feel like I'm standing right next to her.

I knock again. I'm still worried about Ava. I'm worried that I've done something irreparably wrong, that Iris will never let me speak to her daughter again. I considered giving her one of Jess's dolls as a peace offering, an olive branch of sorts, but then I remembered that the marionettes were probably what scared Ava off in the first place. Instead, I hold the brand-new turquoise leotard from Jess's room in one hand and a bottle of red wine in the other, Ava's umbrella sticking out of my back pocket.

"Charles." Iris finally opens the door, warm yellow light

spilling out from the house. She stands on her tiptoes to wrap her arms around me, a hug that lasts for several moments.

"It's good to see you, Charles. Come in and make yourself at home. I'm just finishing up the risotto," Iris says. I follow her into the house, hanging up my coat but leaving on my hat. The interior is simple and cozy, a well-worn couch sitting in front of the fireplace, a kitchen that smells like garlic and Parmesan cheese. I hand Iris the wine and she pours out two glasses. I stand by the counter and watch her cook.

"I checked at the hospital but I didn't find any medical records for you. I'll keep looking, though," Iris says. She tastes the risotto and then adds more salt and basil to the pan.

"And what happens if you don't find them?"

"Well, there are a couple options for next steps. I would recommend seeing a neurologist, getting an MRI. But first we would want to make sure you have health insurance coverage because otherwise that's going to be very expensive. If you don't have insurance, there are some clinics I can look into."

I think about my father, about the exhibition of the schizophrenic man. "Iris, if they do find something wrong, or if they find that I have some sort of psychological condition as opposed to a physical one . . . could they keep me there?"

Iris scoops the risotto into bowls, steam billowing up into her face. She shakes her head. "Against your will? No, they can't do that unless you pose an imminent danger to yourself or others."

I pause for a moment, still feeling unsettled. "Iris, were you surprised when I disappeared?"

"Surprised? I guess yes and no. I was worried, of course, worried that something had happened to you . . ."

"But?"

"But you've always been a bit unpredictable, a bit spontaneous."

"What do you mean?"

"Nothing too significant. Just that you weren't necessarily the type to tell us if you were going out of town, and sometimes you would be at home but wouldn't answer the door for a couple days. Geniuses are eccentric. Everybody says that."

"I'm sorry." I feel myself blushing, the blood pooling into my cheeks. "I hope I haven't been too inconsiderate."

"No, you've been just fine. We both love you, Charles."

"Six months, though."

"That's a long time," Iris agrees. "I don't know where you were, Charles, but something happened. I can't exactly put a finger on it. You seem different."

I hear music playing from the other room, Tchaikovsky's *Swan Lake*. Ava must be practicing for her dance class.

"Ava, dinner's ready! Come say hi to Charles!" Iris calls out over her shoulder.

"No!" Ava yells from the other room, slamming the door, and I can tell that I'm still not in her good graces.

"I brought this for Ava." I gesture to the leotard. "I didn't mean to, but I think I must have said something to upset her."

Iris stirs some fresh thyme into the risotto. "That's sweet of you, Charles. She'll love it. Did you know that turquoise is her favorite color? She used to have a turquoise leotard, but then she left it at the studio one day and we haven't been able to find one since."

"Well, I certainly hope she likes it . . . do you have any

idea what might have upset her? I really didn't mean to say anything wrong."

Iris sits down at the table. She gestures for me to sit across from her. We tap our wine glasses together, and then she gives a short sigh. "Look, Charles, I know we've all been through a lot and that Ava means the world to you, and that sometimes it's easy to accidentally let things slip out that you don't mean."

"That I don't mean?"

"That aren't true." Iris bites her lower lip in a way I can tell is habitual. "Charles, when you first were getting to know us, and Ava told you about Rory and what happened to him, you told her that your father had died too, that your parents had died in a car crash when you were eighteen."

It takes a moment to sink in, and then it hits me why Ava is so upset.

"I understand, Charles. Julie and Jess had just disappeared and it's only natural that you were looking for a way to connect."

"I lied to her."

"She'll be okay. Her feelings are hurt, but we all make mistakes sometimes." Iris squeezes my shoulder, then smiles. "Dinner's ready. Why don't you set the table for the two of us? I imagine Ava's going to eat in her room."

I take the silverware and the plates from the counter, setting them on placemats decorated with little dancing ballerinas. I appreciate Iris's kindness and consideration, but I also don't understand why I would've lied to Ava. It seems out of character, and I can't believe I wouldn't have realized that such a significant lie would be sure to backfire.

I wait for Iris to serve the risotto. My gaze drifts across the living room to a glass shelf filled with vintage model cars, Corvettes and Thunderbirds and even a few Model Ts. But of all the cars, my eyes are most drawn to one in particular, a 1971 Mercedes-Benz sedan, brown exterior, beige interior. A perfectly average car, except that it leaves me feeling queasy. I know that car, and then I picture him, my father, sitting behind the wheel, leaning back, smoking Lucky Strike cigarettes with my mother curled up in the seat next to him.

October 22, 1996

Age Eighteen

Charles sits at the small wooden desk in his dorm room, working quietly and methodically on a problem set for genetics. His room is sparse, austere—a thin twin mattress with gray bedding, a dresser filled with folded socks and shirts, a poster of the periodic table of elements above the desk. Charles stands and walks over to the window to try to push it open farther. Although it's late October, the weather is unseasonably warm for Northern California. Charles wears checkered boxers and a Star Trek T-shirt. A pair of navy pants and a white dress shirt lie draped over the head of the bed. He has the radio tuned to the World Series, the Yankees versus the Braves, although Charles doesn't really care about the outcome.

He told his parents there was no need to come for the weekend.

It was a long drive and there wasn't much to show them. Besides, the campus would be overrun with other parents dawdling around. But Charles's mother insisted on coming anyway, and that was that. Charles certainly couldn't tell her the truth, that he wished they would never visit, that he was tired of his father being sick and of his mother pretending everything was fine. He wishes Julie were coming instead. He hasn't seen her for three months now, and even though they talk all the time, he wants nothing more than to see her face, to look into her eyes, to hold her in his arms. The last time they spoke, she said she had something to tell him. Something she wanted to wait to share until they were together.

Charles gets up for a glass of water and checks the clock over the dresser. He was so absorbed in his problem set that only now is he realizing his parents are over two hours late. Just then, Charles hears a knock on the door.

"One moment!" he calls out, yanking on his pants. The shirt will have to wait.

When Charles opens the door, however, it's not his parents but the dorm's residential advisor, an awkward girl with a blond ponytail and freckled cheeks. She tries to speak but every time she opens her mouth, nothing comes out.

"What's going on?"

"There's a policeman here. He wants to talk to you." As Charles follows the girl down the hall, his mind runs through all of the offenses he committed in the last week or so. He's not a bad person but a mischievous one, and he and his cohorts in the engineering department have spent the past several months one-upping each other with various pranks. Could it be about the swimming pool? Or the sheep brain gone missing?

The police officer takes off his hat and clutches it in his hands when he sees Charles turning the corner. His face is pale, ghastly. And instantly Charles feels sick. He wants nothing more than to run the other way. But instead Charles stands there, entrapped, as the officer tells him that there's been an accident. The officer continues talking, but Charles doesn't hear any of it. He sinks to his knees and feels his chest crushing in on itself. Soon everything turns black.

The funeral takes place the day after Halloween, the weather having turned dark and morose, a sudden cold front. Several of the graves are still strewn with toilet paper from the night before. Charles has hardly spoken a word over the last week or so. He cannot believe his parents are dead. Charles remains fixated on the broad-shouldered man in the back of the crowd, holding a photograph of Charles's mother. He imagines his mother resting peacefully in this man's arms, kissing his thin, soft lips. He thinks of Plato and the allegory of the cave, of how nothing about his life has been any more real than a couple shadows cast against a wall, and what is worse is that he understands, he understands why his mother made the decisions she did, why she looked beyond her marriage for affection, for love. At the same time, Charles knows that every day he is becoming more and more like his father, and he fears that he's destined to be left behind as well.

"ARE YOU ALL RIGHT?"

Iris has her hand against my forehead. My face is damp, a trickle of sweat running down my temple. I seem to have dropped the model car on the hardwood floor. The front has cracked apart, little bits of glass from the headlights scattered around it.

"I didn't lie."

"What?"

"I didn't lie to Ava. About my father."

Iris throws the car in the trash and wets a paper towel. "It's okay, Charles, it doesn't matter what you said."

"My parents are dead, Iris. They died in a car crash when I was eighteen."

Iris crouches, wiping up the glass. When I say this, she stops what she's doing and sets down the paper towel.

"And the man living at your house?" she asks. She frowns slightly. I sit down at the table, folding my hands together. I see my parents' graves, two flat, gray headstones, their lives reduced to names and dates. The walls feel like they're narrowing around me, tilting, about to fall over.

"I don't know," I finally say. "I don't know who the man is."

PART II

May 4, 1996

Age Eighteen

The night air is warm like fresh honey, the grass calm beneath his bare feet. The stadium feels monolithic, and Charles imagines he is Julius Caesar, carrying his empress across treacherous terrain. Julie giggles at his chivalry, although eventually she demands to be let down so that she can run around the field herself, doing cartwheels and somersaults, twirling around the football field's yellow end post. Her dress flies around her, emerald-green fabric overlapping on itself so that it looks like forest leaves. Normally, when there's a game, the stadium is packed with at least five hundred people, yelling and hooting and waving their arms beneath bright fluorescent lights. But tonight, it's all theirs. Everyone else is inside the gym, disco balls spinning, streamers flying, music bumping, "This Is How We Do It" and "Gangsta's Paradise" and "I'm Every Woman" filtering out across the field.

Charles has tried his best to be a proper prom date. He donned a tuxedo for the first time in his life, trimmed the dead ends off his shoulder-length hair, shaved the scruff, and slapped his cheeks with cologne. He arrived at Julie's house with a proper corsage made from white roses and baby's breath, sliding it onto her slender wrist, placing a blanket on the passenger seat of his father's car in case

Julie got cold. But the prom itself seemed impossible. It was too loud to talk, too crowded to see, and it soon became clear to Charles that with all of his twisting and turning and flailing out of time with the music, he was most definitely the worst dancer in the entire room. After three songs, he ripped the knees of his pants, after five, he elbowed a girl in the nose, and after six, overwhelmed by the noise and the sweat, by the guilt he felt for the toes he crushed, Charles was sure he was going to faint if they didn't duck outside.

On the football field, Julie sneaks up on Charles and pounces on his back. They spin in a circle, swirling until they are both on the ground, dizzy and breathing hard, the stars pirouetting angels in the night sky. Charles slips off his jacket and lays it over Julie's shoulders. His hand inches infinitesimally closer to Julie's until his pinky finger is touching hers. She takes his hand. And then, before he knows what he's doing, Charles leans over and kisses Julie. It is his first kiss. Ever. The kiss is wet and strange and soft and wonderful. Charles pulls away, wanting to tell Julie everything he feels for her, how much he loves her, how he cannot imagine being lonely when he is with her. But instead, he sneezes, a large, elephant sneeze right in Julie's face, and they laugh, and the moment is over, and he realizes he doesn't know how to say anything.

"I can't believe you're leaving. What am I going to do without you here?" Julie says.

"It's not for a while. Not for a few months."

"But still . . ."

Julie pulls up several blades of grass, creating a little nest in her palm. Charles tucks his knees against himself.

"You should call CalArts. Tell them you changed your mind. It's not too late, and then at least we'd be in the same state."

"I wish, but I can't afford it."

"There must be a—"

"It's fine. Really. I'll stay here, work and save up for two years, get some classes out of the way, and then I'll transfer and it won't matter."

Charles looks into Julie's eyes. "Promise me you'll visit this fall?"

"You're not even going to miss me. Not after the first week or two. You'll have a bunch of new college friends, and your brain will be so full of biology and chemistry and physics that you won't have time to think about girls."

"But you promise you will?"

Julie gives Charles a peck on the cheek. "Of course."

Charles opens his mouth, wanting to profess his true feelings for her, but all the words get stuck in his throat and he lets out an awkward croak instead. Julie doesn't notice. She's looking up at the stars again, lost in thought.

"I can't believe Steve isn't here," she says finally.

"Yeah, I know. I mean, I know why he had to do it, but still. I thought we were all going to have one last summer together."

"I hope he finds a cute boy. I hope he finds a way to be happy."

Steve had a bad few months. His parents kicked him out. Sometimes he slept at Charles' house, sometimes at Julie's, mostly at his uncle's. He became quiet. He lost weight. His grades dropped. Then one morning there was just a note on Charles' doorstep, in Steve's handwriting: "Took my life's savings. Don't try to look for me. Sorry . . ." Charles was disappointed but not surprised.

"I'm so afraid of losing you, Julie. I don't know what I would do."

"You won't lose me." Julie wraps her arms around Charles' chest, resting her chin against his shoulder. "I promise, you won't lose me."

"I'm going to hold you to that," Charles says. Suddenly he's grinning, and he rolls Julie over, kissing her again and again.

THE SUN FEELS INVASIVE AND DANGEROUS AS I SHIELD my eyes, stepping out onto my porch, a briefcase slung over a sore right shoulder. I tried to climb the wooden trellis to the second story of the house, but halfway up, my foot slipped against the crumbling plaster and I tumbled down onto the lawn. I was lucky to have only gotten a few bruises and scrapes, narrowly avoiding the thicket of rose bushes. I'll have to figure out another way up to the second floor.

It rained all last night, but the puddles have evaporated and the lawns are laundered dry, as if the rain never existed. Little children run and squeal through sprinklers as dads recline in lawn chairs, wearing polo shirts and leather deck shoes. They reach up to kiss young wives who set fresh lemonade and sugar cookies on patio tables. I glance back at my house. A plank of wood is missing from the window to the right of the front door. I wonder if one of the neighborhood kids pried it off, if they dared each other to peek in through the window, if they've seen the old man, if he's a ghost to them, a specter, if he's less than human to the outside world too. I doubt the old man has noticed the sunlight streaming in through the crack, and I doubt he's noticed that it's spring and that the birds are chirping and the kids are playing and that all around families are rejoicing together. I don't know what to do with him. Even if he's not my father, the resemblance is there, an uncle, a grandfather, a cousin on my father's side. He's mine, my blood, and there's nothing else for me to do.

I rub my thumb against the prom photo still tucked into my left palm, Julie nuzzled into the crook of Charles's arm, wearing his tuxedo jacket, her head pushing his bow tie askew, their smiles all flash. It's the only photo I could find of Julie and Charles together.

I keep thinking of this past Charles in the third person. It's like I'm watching some sort of majestic, surreal film featuring an actor who looks identical to me. But I can't enter this film, there's a screen preventing it, and as much as I'd like to stick one foot in, it's impossible. Because it's not my film. It's not my life. Not anymore, at least.

"Charles!" a voice calls out, and I turn to see Iris, watering the azaleas on her front porch. "Where are you going in such a hurry?"

"Was I walking fast?"

"Like your life depended on it."

"Oh, I didn't realize. I guess I'm just nervous. I'm going back to work."

"Charles, you can't walk there, it's three miles away, and in this weather, you're going to drown in your own sweat before you make it." Iris shakes out the last few drops from her watering can onto the grass, rolling up the muddy cuffs of the men's overalls she wears. "Come on, it's my day off and I was going downtown anyway to run some errands. Just let me get changed and then I'll give you a ride. What time are they expecting you?"

"There's no rush." I follow Iris into the house. The truth is that they're not expecting me. I don't even really know where I'm going. I had a dream last night where I paced back and forth in front of a generic beige building with the address 1247 Shelby Ave., wearing a lab coat with a bloody handprint on the pocket. When I woke up this morning, some part of me knew that's where I needed to go next. The blood, I hoped, was just a product of my imagination. My plan was to wander toward downtown and find the lab. While this plan partially resulted from the fact that there was no computer at the house I could use to look up a map on Google, no phone that I could use to call a cab, I also liked the idea of exploring Hillston on foot. Maybe I hoped that investigating my surroundings might provide some sort of useful information. And maybe I liked the idea of getting lost. But I was being naïve. I should go with Iris. I needed to continue to be practical, to rely on logic if I was going to make any progress.

"You ready?" Iris asks. She's put on chinos and a clean linen blouse. I startle, dropping the photo of Julie and Charles onto the kitchen's tiled floor. I scramble to my knees, picking it up with a quick swoop. If Iris notices, she pretends she hasn't.

The neighborhood feels foreign as Iris drives us down the street. The evidence so far suggests that I grew up here, that there should be memories everywhere. Instead, everything feels off. The blue of the sky is too saturated, the neighbors' smiles threatening. There's a breeze blowing and yet the air is still. I feel dozens of sets of eyes on me, although I can't tell whose eyes they are.

But then we approach a house down at the far end of the

street, a house overgrown with green ivy, a gray thatched roof leaning low. A cobblestone pathway leads up to the front door. A colony of hang-headed scarecrows, worn with age, congregates in the yard. The front windows are made of stained glass, casting bright, slanted shadows across the living room's hardwood floor. I don't think I've ever seen a house with so many stained glass windows before. A plume of smoke curls up from behind the house, and a warm feeling rises in my chest.

November 7, 1984

Age Six

The young boy Charles runs as fast as he can, although he can no longer remember from whom or what. The lenses of his glasses begin to fog up. He pauses for a moment to catch his breath. Suddenly he realizes where he is and who's watching him.

"Hello there," says Mrs. Hollingberry, glancing up at Charles from beneath the wide brim of her gardening hat. She notices Charles staring at the strange vegetable in her left hand, the one she has just pulled from the ground. She smiles. "It's a root vegetable. Yucca."

Charles continues to stare. He has never seen somebody who looks at all like her. His parents own pastel sweaters, khaki slacks, and straight-cut skirts that pinch at the waist. But this woman wears deep violet robes that cover her shoulders, mint green tights that cling to her slim legs, goldenrod slippers turned up at the toe, all of which shimmer in the grinning sunlight. Standing in the midst of the garden, her shoes slightly sunken into the earth, she almost seems to be growing herself, her feet rooted into the soil. Smoke rises from a stone pit behind her, and Charles expects the smell of meat, of hamburgers and hotdogs roasting over hot coals. Instead, it's something else, an herb, a floral scent, and as he breathes in, he feels himself grow calm.

"Would you like to come in for a snack?" Mrs. Hollingberry asks. Charles hesitates. His parents have always warned him very strictly not to trust strangers, and some part of him is sure that his mother has a specific dislike for this woman. Mrs. Hollingberry has been mentioned in passing, at dinner, on the way to school. But there's something compelling about this woman as well, something irresistible about the yucca and the clothing and the strange smell drifting through the air around him.

"Sure," he says. Mrs. Hollingberry takes his hand. As Charles walks inside, it's as if he's entered a different universe. His feeling of serenity edges away. Marionettes hang down from the ceilings, gazing at him with wide eyes and impish grins. Plastic dolls lie in dismembered piles, hundreds of arms and legs, heads peeking through the gaps to try to gasp for air. The strands of the carpet are crusted over with old paint, clay, and mud.

Charles and Mrs. Hollingberry pass by a dining room. The table and chairs are much too high for any normal human being, perhaps seven, eight feet tall. A machine sitting on top of the table projects images of food onto the ceiling, turkey and mashed potatoes and cranberry sauce. Another room sits completely empty except for a miniaturist painting all along the bottom edge of the walls, detailing the entirety of human history. There's a strange pattern to the images, and years later, while looking at the same painting, Charles would realize it was done in a wholly reversible fashion, the images constructed such that moving in either direction from a single point, history would appear to both progress and regress in time.

In the next room, the floor is made wholly of puzzle pieces composing a gigantic photograph of an eye. A single piece is missing, right over the place where the pupil would have been. Two men dressed in silk pajama pants wander in with bowls of oatmeal and sit down to eat. Each has a long beard trailing down his chest. They stare at Charles as he walks by.

Charles's throat closes up. He's sure that Mrs. Hollingberry has just tightened her grip. He counts silently in his head. He has decided that he will rip away from Mrs. Hollingberry and escape back through the garden. He should have listened to his parents, such a foolish mistake.

"Julie?" Mrs. Hollingberry says. Charles must have closed his eyes at some point. He opens them to discover a young girl standing before him, her face surrounded by dark ringlets. "Julie, there's somebody I'd like you to meet."

Charles looks at Julie. Julie looks at Charles. Neither one can look away.

"Charles?" Skyscrapers rise around us like sentries as we approach downtown. We pass by a school yard, a swarm of kids in orange and yellow jerseys running back and forth down the basketball court. Women sit outside coffee shops, eating croissants, drinking tea, laughing as though everything is fine.

"Charles?"

"Mm-hmm?"

"There's something I've been meaning to ask you."

"About what?"

Iris catches the look in my eyes. "Oh, it's not about anything important . . ."

"What?"

"Well, it's actually about the leotard you gave Ava. She's so in love with it, that turquoise color. It's exactly like the one she used to have. I was wondering where you bought it. You know how it is with kids—the more she loves it, the more likely it is that it'll get lost."

"I don't know."

"Charles—"

"I'm not sure where I got it."

Iris gives a maternal smile. "You know, there's no right or wrong answer."

I pause. "From Jess's bedroom."

"Pardon?"

"I got it from Jess's bedroom. It's never been worn. I found it folded on top of the dresser. It made me think of Ava."

"Oh." Silence. Iris feigns an unexpected fascination with the road in front of her. She stares straight ahead, lifting her right hand to brush her hair behind her ear.

"I'm sorry, maybe that's weird. Maybe I shouldn't have done that." I turn toward Iris. There is a strength to her figure in profile, her jaw set, her nose sharp and defined, a line or two running across her forehead, a beauty that has gone through tragedy, that has led a difficult life but that has persisted through it anyway. "Look, Iris, I know we may have had this conversation. It's just that, I was wondering—well, do you know what I did with all the photographs in my house?"

I expect Iris's expression to soften, but instead, in a voice just neutral enough to be cold, she says, "I don't know, Charles. They were gone by the time we met you, by the time Rory . . ." She trails off. Her eyes are somewhere else, perhaps lurking through memories with Rory at her side, only for him to disappear when she flashes back to reality. She stomps her foot on the brake to avoid running a red light.

"That's it," I say.

"What?"

"That's the building. You can drop me off here. Thanks, and don't worry about picking me up. I can walk home." Before Iris can respond, I'm out of the car, dashing across the street, clutching my briefcase against my chest. There it is. 1247 Shelby Ave., as bland and beige as they come. Professional. Sterile. I take a step forward and stand in the entryway for several moments, mesmerized as I watch the mirrored glass doors slide open and closed. I unclasp the briefcase for the first time. It's empty inside except for a pair of tortoiseshell glasses. I reach in, take out the glasses and adjust them on my nose. Everything is slightly clearer than before.

I look at my reflection in the sliding doors. My head is mostly healed now. The only sign of any possible accident is a slight bruise on the back of my neck. I wonder if I'll recognize anybody or anything, how they'll react to me. I should've called. I should've called ahead, but I can't think of walking away now. I have to do it. I have to show up.

A deep breath. I enter the building. The soles of my shoes

squeak against the gray-blue linoleum. A woman in a business suit sits in the lobby, reading the *Washington Post* and drinking a coffee. She glances up vaguely as I walk by and then returns to her article, swinging her foot in time with the smooth jazz music that echoes from hidden speakers. I check the building directory, then press the button outside of the elevator. Of all the companies named, the only one that seems like a potential is Genutech, listed on the fifth floor.

The orange arrow glows brightly, followed by a ding. I can't help but feel like the elevator is growing narrower as it rises. I undo the first button at the top of my shirt and try not to hyperventilate. When I exit the elevator, there's a set of double doors immediately in front of me, bookended on either side by a large potted plant. A red light pulsates to the left of the door, and a little sign makes it clear I need a security badge. I have a hunch. I open the briefcase and run my fingers along the inside. One of my fingers catches. There's a pocket in the lining along the back. Inside the pocket is a wallet, a cell phone, several tissues, a pack of mint gum. Before I reach for the wallet, I take out the cell phone, press several buttons at once. If this is my phone, then it has my contacts in it. I can't get it to turn on, however. The battery and the SIM card are missing.

I then take out the wallet, thin brown leather worn at the corners. I check inside. There's a driver's license, several credit cards, a debit card, a few dollars, and a security badge with a barcode at the bottom. I slide out the driver's license, holding it up to the light. The photograph must be at least ten years old. My blond hair is buzzed short, my blue eyes gleaming, and I have a crooked half smile, like I'm not sure how to pose. My full name is spelled out, Charles Alexander Lang, my permanent address listed as 153 Maple Road, Hillston, WA 98409. A new piece of information—my birthday, December 5, 1977, which would indeed make me thirty-four years old. I take out the security badge next. The expression of this man, in contrast, is stiff and mechanical, but there's no doubt it's me. I hold the security badge up to the red light. There's a loud click as the doors unlock. The hallway extends forth, an infinite mirrored corridor converging on itself. Why do they need so much security? What could Genutech have to hide? I reach the next set of doors, hold my thumb up to a scanner. Nothing. I try again. Nothing. Finally I turn my thumb over so that it goes in upside down. The device purrs and shines a blue light as the doors swing open, revealing another long open space with offices branching off to the sides. I step inside and instantly notice a familiar stain across the carpet, huge and sprawling, the color somewhere between brown and dark burgundy.

January 31, 2010

Age Thirty-Two

Charles tears through the office, leaving armfuls of shredded paper in his wake. Shattered bits of glass are strewn across the carpet. Chemicals leak from the tanks along the wall; water puddles on the floor. Something translucent struggles in one of the puddles, some sort of sea life. Frayed wires sizzle in the water. A flat-screened modem lies cracked in two pieces. Charles is nothing but anger and despair. His boss, Peter, paces back and forth in the corner, gaunt in a suit jacket with his white, thinning hair and spectacles. He speaks quietly, urgently into a cell phone. The skin around his right eye is raised, red fading to black and blue. He glances furtively at Charles, who is now muttering to himself and emptying several drawers' worth of files at his feet. Charles rips one sheet after the other, sinking down to his knees among a mountain of shredded paper.

A security guard bursts through the double doors and then slows, taking in the destruction around him. He turns his head to his shoulder, presses the button on his walkie-talkie and radios for backup. The guard approaches Charles, gently touches his shoulder. Charles flinches, turns to look at the guard. His glasses are chipped and smudged, his eyes clouded over.

⁂

FOR THE FIRST TIME I THINK THAT MAYBE THIS REALLY IS me. I feel more like this Charles from my memories than I ever have before.

"Charles, is that you?"

I'm standing in the same room as in the memory, a central corridor with an antiseptic feeling opening onto offices and labs, the mirrored windows lining the passageway giving a constant, uncomfortable awareness of oneself. Anything that I may have damaged has been neatly repaired, with all hints of past destruction tucked behind and beneath the flawless tables and carpets. If previously there were water tanks against the walls, they have since been moved, with only the slightest discoloration of the wallpaper giving any suggestion of their prior existence. There's a marble countertop with coffee, tea, and pastries in one corner, a water cooler, several leather couches and a table with magazines and newspapers.

I blink. There is no carpet, no stain left. Hardwood floors have replaced the carpet. The room looks like a doctor's office, anything dangerous long since removed and locked away. I still feel shaken by the last memory. I wonder what exactly caused such distress. I wonder if it had something to do with Julie and Jess, if it had something to do with my absence as well.

Peter stands before me, holding a clipboard in one hand, a pen in the other. He's lanky with a beakish nose and small bird eyes, his limbs too long and angular for his body, like stalks of wheat. His white shirt is pressed and starched, his thick, black-framed glasses without a smudge, his pants perfectly creased, his shoes recently shined. His eyes linger. I would expect Peter to seem more surprised, perhaps taken aback at my unexpected appearance. Instead, he takes me in with a studied expression, with the sort of calm a physician maintains for even his sickest patients, a calm that is mechanical in a way.

"It's good to see you back, Charles," Peter says, extending a hand, and I give it a firm shake. "Shall we get you set up?"

"Um, sure. There's nothing else I need to do first? I wasn't expecting, well, it's been so long—"

"It's up to you, Charles. Whatever you want."

"Of course, then. Of course." I follow Peter as he starts out at a clip down the corridor. I practically have to jog to keep up with him. His shoes against the hardwood are like a metronome to my thoughts, but my mind soon pulls away, diving and swirling. I know that I should consider myself lucky, that I should accept the status quo, but I want to know more, so badly that the questions blister like heartburn deep in my chest. Peter stops to take a key out of his pocket and before I can help it, the words spill out of me.

"Peter, what happened to me? I've been gone, haven't I, about six months or so?"

"It's all been taken care of, Charles."

"But, you know what happened to me? Where I've been? Because I don't remember. I know I shouldn't tell you this, but I don't remember at all."

Peter unlocks the door. He pauses to give me a bemused half smile. "Come in. I'd be more than happy to explain."

My office looks more like an aquarium than anything else. The white walls reflect a blue luminescence as fluorescent bulbs light up the tanks, enormous tanks of water that extend from the floor to the ceiling on three out of the four sides of the room. Each of the tanks is subdivided into sections, and in each section there's a colony of jellyfish floating around. The bell and tendrils of the jellyfish are translucent, and inside each of the bells is a radiant red bulb held within a gelatinous tube. The only other light in the room is the glow of the computer screens. They are mounted on top of an enormous black printer and line the fourth wall. I reach my fingers up to the glass, imagining if I could touch one of the swaying jellyfish, what it would feel like. Peter flips on the rest of the overhead lights and the room feels less eerie, less supernatural.

"*Turritopsis dohrnii.* The immortal jellyfish," Peter says. I realize that I already know this somehow.

"The only known case of a metazoan that's capable of reverting completely to a sexually immature state after having reached sexual maturity. Cell transdifferentiation—the jellyfish can alter the differentiated state of a cell and transform it into a new cell," I say. I retrieve the knowledge from some far-off niche in my brain.

"That's right." Peter nods. He studies me again. I feel like a lab specimen. I sit down on one of the metal benches by the tanks and wonder what it's like to be a jellyfish, if they ever wish they were more anchored. Peter sits down across from me, his feet rooted against the floor.

"You had a brain aneurysm, Charles. The blood vessel ruptured and you nearly died. You were in and out of consciousness for about a month and then spent the next several months in the hospital for rehabilitation. The doctors said that you would continue to have some issues with your episodic memory but that it will eventually return. I apologize for not staying with you the night I drove you home. I thought that you might enjoy some privacy." Peter puts a hand on my shoulder, in a gesture that seems more artificial than genuine.

"And the old man who's living with me? Do you know who he is?"

Peter's eyes twitch upward for a moment, as if he's trying to decide what to say. "I didn't meet him. I would imagine a relative of some sort?"

Some gut instinct tells me that Peter is lying, either in whole or in part, but I have no idea why. I decide not to press him. I don't want to ruin this.

"And you're okay with this? With me working in the lab? I'm clearly not the person I used to be," I say.

Peter smiles. "I would have you no other way than you are. You're brilliant, Charles, beyond brilliant. Just look around you if you're unsure." The minimal wall space around the computers is covered with degrees and certificates, detailing and confirming my accomplishments.

"And if you can figure out a way to make our stem cells transdifferentiate," Peter continues, "well, there would be almost no limit to our ability to renew dead or damaged tissue and organs in humans."

I raise my hand to one of the awards, a certificate pressed in a frame, and when my fingertips touch the cool glass, a tingling sensation spreads through my arms and legs.

February 6, 2001

Age Twenty-Three

Charles stands before a crowded auditorium. His face is still too young for his age, his cheeks too rosy, his glasses too big. He looks like a teenage boy wearing his father's suit, without the clownishness of a child but lacking the bulkier body to fill out the shoulders and waist. His hair is shorter now, trimmed, an attempt at adulthood.

Charles should be smiling. Applause echoes through the auditorium as if millions of little girls are tap dancing. Another man with deep wrinkles and a fleshy neck stands next to Charles, shaking his hand as he gives him a framed certificate and a gold medal. The certificate is made out to Charles Lang, in recognition of his achievements in genetics and molecular biology. The man then takes a sheath of notes from his breast pocket, begins to speak. But the speech sounds garbled to Charles. He cannot focus on the man, the words. He cannot focus on anybody but Julie, Julie who he has not spoken to in four years, Julie who he imagines sitting in the front row of the audience, cheering and applauding. This moment should mean everything to Charles. He's the youngest researcher to have ever received such an award. The award guarantees success, security, wealth, and a place in history as one of the most influential scientists of the twenty-first century.

Yet Charles can think of nothing besides Julie's dark, flowing hair and silky skin. He feels an emotion for her that is beyond attraction, something that is caring and sweetness and longing and thirst, a desire for his chest to always be against hers and for his arms to be around her sturdy shoulders. And as the man garbles on behind him, voice booming, arms gesticulating, Charles realizes that he is in love with Julie, and that nothing else in the world can compare. After all this time, after all these years, he cannot believe he has never told her this before.

"CHARLES?" PETER SAYS, AND I GLANCE UP, CATCHING my reflection in Peter's glasses. My eyes are pink around the edges, dark circles underneath. Four years? Why would I have gone so long without talking to Julie? Did we have a falling out somewhere along the way?

"Charles?"

"Mmm?"

"How does it all feel?"

"I don't know. Exciting. Overwhelming. And what happens if I can't replicate this cell transdifferentiation? What then?"

Peter folds his fingers together.

"Do you know when the vaccine was invented?" he asks.

"Of course." I don't actually know.

Peter paces around the office and then looks up. As he speaks, his voice is detached, barren, as if he's reciting from a grocery list.

"You know, there was originally a great deal of tension regarding my takeover of the company and my active involvement in your research projects. I won't say who in particular opposed it, but several of the scientists here thought I was completely over my head with my background in scientific history and consulting, that I should leave the research part to the 'actual' scientists. They thought all I was good for was the funding, nothing more.

"But none of them knew who invented the vaccine, British physician and scientist Edward Jenner. On May 14, 1796, Jenner's patient, James Phipps, received the first smallpox inoculation, an inoculation that would go on to save millions of lives." The name Jenner sounds familiar.

"But Jenner was only able to make such a discovery because of the scientific and historical stepping stones that came before him. He couldn't have developed his vaccine if it weren't for Lady Mary Wortley Montagu in the early 1700s, who demonstrated to the British that variolation, or deliberately infecting healthy individuals with small amounts of smallpox, could make these individuals immune to the disease later in life. And before Lady Montagu was ever born, the Chinese and the Indians had been practicing approximations of variolation for nearly two thousand years."

"Right," I say. Jenner. There's something there, at the tip of my tongue, memories that leave a bad taste in my mouth. Peter paces back and forth, as a professor might if he were just about to deliver the thesis to his lecture.

"You see, it is my belief that there is a paradigm for scientific breakthroughs, a recurring, algorithmic process that has occurred throughout history. And this algorithm that I have deciphered will enable societies to engage in more fine-tuned research practices and consequently lead to very accurate predictions about when a given scientific breakthrough is likely to occur. It's my job to analyze these historical figures and statistics, and they point to you. You are the next step."

The information comes to me, sour and heavy in the back of my throat. "Wasn't Edward Jenner the one who first tested his smallpox vaccine on an eight-year-old boy?"

"Yes, and his discovery went on to eradicate one of the most destructive diseases from our planet."

"Jenner vaccinated the boy without his father's permission and then exposed him to smallpox. It would be like exposing a child today to Ebola or anthrax. The boy was violently sick for ten days. He could have died."

"Sacrifices have to be made for the sake of scientific progress," Peter says quietly. "It is illogical for our sentimental attachment to one life to get in the way of our potential to save many lives in the future."

"And if I don't want to make sacrifices? If I don't want to be compared to a man who nearly killed a young child?"

Peter pauses. "You are going to be one of the most famous and prolific scientists who has ever lived, Charles. It doesn't matter what you want."

January 17, 2011

Age Thirty-Three

Charles stands in a laboratory very late at night. There are crow's feet pinching at the corners of his eyes from lack of sleep. A thin stream of fluorescence filters through a crack in the ceiling above, reflecting off one of the metal surgical tables. Somewhere at a distance a janitor pushes a container of cloudy mop water down a hallway. One of the wheels is off-kilter and squeaks.

The lab is dark except for the single sliver of light from above. Several empty coffee cups lay discarded by the waste bin. It seems like Charles isn't supposed to be in the room at this time of night. Perhaps not at all. His movements are careful and discreet and he has also pushed one of the file cabinets against the door, presumably to prevent anyone else from entering. There are no windows to this room and the door is very short, only about five and a half feet tall. The room smells like cleaning alcohol and expired flesh.

Humming against the back wall is what appears to be some sort of large metal refrigerator, the outdated design and collecting grime suggesting that it's an archaic model or that it has at least seen better days. Charles washes his hands under hot water, puts on a pair of latex gloves, slides a mask over his face. He makes several starts toward the refrigerator, stopping, starting again. He rocks back and forth on his heels, breathing rapidly, until finally he tears off the latex gloves and mask and begins to bite his fingernails in a ravenous fashion. He bites them until they start to bleed.

Charles releases a deep exhalation and disposes of the soiled gloves and mask, then commences the process again. He winces as he places his hands under the hot water. This time he approaches more slowly. He allows himself time to breathe and wait. He's both very excited and very scared.

Charles's hand quivers as he reaches for the handle. When he opens the door, he immediately releases it, jumps back, gagging, blasted by a wave of warm air that reeks of decay. The machine is not a refrigerator after all but seems to be some sort of incubation chamber, harboring two putrid, barely alive bodies. The larger one raises its head, wheezing through its deteriorating lips, skin peeling off of its cheeks. It attempts a smile, a smile that causes blood to leak from the corners of its mouth. The smaller one lays nearly immobile on the floor, its mutilated limbs curled under its stomach. Its breathing comes out in short, quiet hisses. The smaller one becomes aware of Charles's presence, as Charles sits on the floor, covering his eyes and continuing to gag.

"Daddy!" the small one squeals with delight, although the word

is mangled, barely decipherable for what it is. It tries to pull itself up, grabbing at the bottom of Charles's lab coat and leaving a bloody handprint before falling to the floor once more. Charles raises his head, attempts to look at this small, emaciated creature before him, this creature who is supposed to be his daughter. But in the end he can't. He can't look at the creature, nor can he shut the door. All he can do is sit, sit and hope for everything to be over soon.

WHEN I BECOME AWARE OF THE LAB AGAIN, I CAN STILL smell the stench of the decaying bodies, nightmarish bodies, impossible bodies, the warm, bloody handprint stark in contrast to the white of my lab coat. I'm crouched on the floor, in a squatting position. Peter sits at one of the computers, transcribing various numbers and figures. He scratches his ear in an absent way, completely tuned in to whatever it is that he's doing. The bodies and the hidden laboratory feel close, alive, but as I rise to my feet and look around, the remnants of the memory begin to dissipate. I still feel a hopelessness weighing down on me, though, like the air around me has suddenly become denser. I want to convince myself that these terrible bodies were just part of a dream. Everything felt exaggerated, surreal, larger than life. But the details were too minute, the emotions too raw. Whatever awful thing I just experienced was most certainly real.

Peter smiles and hums as he types, an upbeat song from *The Music Man*. I envy him. He seems completely at ease, completely himself, a man whose wholeness has never been subjected to any significant tragedy. I approach Peter, tap him on the shoulder. He startles.

"Didn't realize you were still in here, Charles!"

"I'm sorry for earlier. Maybe I overreacted," I say. I put out a hand for Peter and he reaches out, giving it a nice, firm shake.

"Well then, Human Resources will draft a copy of your contract, benefits, payroll information, etc. that you can come pick up tomorrow. They're around the corner, down the hall. And then you'll be all set for Monday, full lab privileges and such. If you need to start slow, part time, that's fine of course, but any time you can put in we'd be happy to have."

"Peter?"

"What is it, Charles?"

I hesitate. "What if I've already figured it all out? The mimicking of these stem cells, the prolonging of life, but the results are . . . undesirable."

Peter pauses, looks me straight in the eye. We stand frozen for several seconds.

"You always were a funny one, Charles," he says in a deadpan tone. "Very funny. I'll see you tomorrow then."

I leave the office building at dusk after cleaning up the lab a bit, just as the sun is starting to drift down behind the skyscrapers and restaurants, the air like steel in my lungs. I decide to take a more circuitous route home, meandering, exploring. I know that eventually I have to return to the house, to its claustrophobic and stagnant environment, but for now, I'm enjoying the fresh air and the solitude. Worst-case scenario, I can always call a taxi.

There's something too sterile about the lab. It's overcompensating for something dirty and savage underneath the new paint and state-of-the-art technology. I wonder what happened between my mental breakdown two years ago and the memory loss I experienced six months ago. I also don't know what to make of Peter. He's lying about something but I can't tell what.

I focus on the environment around me, the cedars swaying in the wind, children playing basketball at a park, the smells of trash and gasoline, the sounds of car radios and a couple's terse conversation. I stroll aimlessly up and down streets, streets that feel anonymous, each one simply a replication of the last with some minor adjustments. There are neighborhood cafes, pharmacies, dry cleaners, grocery stores. The residential areas are even more homogeneous. I wonder if people ever have trouble distinguishing their own houses from those of their neighbors.

At a certain point, the houses grow farther and fewer between, replaced by long stretches of uncut grass and weeds. It smells more like nature than the city, like fresh leaves and mud. The air grows damp. It's going to rain soon. I stop and look around, trying to imagine what direction might take me back to the house, when I notice a narrow road to the right, curving off into the distance, the asphalt pitted and crumbling. A barrage of emotions washes over me, emotions so intense that I lose my footing for a moment. I feel elation and despair and something even stronger. I've been here before. I've been here many times. I start down the road, past a post office, an antiques shop, a shuttered restaurant, until suddenly, unexpectedly, I'm knocked down to my knees. At first I'm convinced that somebody else did this to me. But as I look around and find myself alone, I realize that the force is internal, an overwhelming nostalgia that I struggle against as I make my way to my feet.

I'm kneeling in front of a small tavern. A dark wooden arch that appears centuries old curves over a set of stairs leading down into the basement. It's the sort of place that doesn't have a name. People have always just known how to find it. I walk down the creaky, dusty steps into a spacious underground room, the walls lined with thick slabs of stone, just as I imagine they would have been in the medieval days. Behind the bar there are at least a dozen wooden barrels of beer stacked one on top of the other. A few hand-carved tables and stools are scattered throughout, and besides an aging couple sitting together and drinking pints of ale, the tavern is empty. Although I know that the space is most likely decorated specifically to evoke the imagined peacefulness of older, simpler times, I also feel an earthy sense of home within these walls. I've been here many times before. I've felt comfortable, safe, and happy while here.

The bartender emerges from behind the barrels, wiping his face with a dirty towel. His face is like a desert scrubland, tufts of beard here and there, his dark hair combed back slick and smooth in comparison. He squints up at me, in a way that makes it difficult for me to know whether or not he's pleased I'm here.

"You want something to drink?" he asks gruffly. I would've expected something friendlier, more familiar.

"Yes, whatever you'd recommend."

He leans down behind the bar for a clean glass and fills it from the tap, golden and frothy. I sit down at the bar, take a sip. It tastes exactly as I imagined it would, like warm, yeasty bread. I've had this beer before.

"Have we met? I used to come here a lot, I think. The name Charles Lang ring a bell?"

The bartender frowns. "I've only worked here for a few months now. The bar changed ownership and the old bartender left cause he didn't like the new guy."

He seems to think this is enough of an explanation and disappears into the back. I sit there in silence, tipping my glass one way and then the other so that I can watch the bubbles shift around. I hear the sink running, the bartender whistling. He seems much happier alone.

A few minutes later, the bartender pops his head back out again. This time, he's holding a photo.

"This you?" he says, sliding a Polaroid across the bar. If I had to guess, I'd say I was in my mid to late twenties. The photograph is in black and white. I'm gazing up, a dark, wandering expression on my face, wearing a white button-down, suspenders, and a pair of charcoal-gray slacks.

"Yeah, that's me." I look sullen, morose.

"Apparently you were a very loyal customer." There's a touch of contempt in his voice for some reason, and he leaves the photograph with me on the countertop.

I pause and then I begin to remember. Every Thursday. Julie and I would come in around five or six. I would be in my work clothes and when I got here, I would take off my tie and undo the top button on my shirt. And then Julie would always come in ten minutes later, and she would be wearing the same purple dress. A ritual. Our ritual.

December 29, 2003

Age Twenty-Six

Charles sits at the bar, finishing off a beer. His tie is slung back over his shoulder. The bartender asks if he would like another. It's a different bartender, twenty pounds heavier and significantly balder, someone of a previous generation. Charles nods. He pushes his glasses back up his nose. They've slid down with sweat. The tavern is warm, warmer than Charles expected. Not that Charles came with expectations. In fact, Charles isn't sure how he even got here in the first place. He was walking home from the lab along his typical route, his mind drifting. The next time he looked up, he was standing in front of the tavern, his coat slouching off his slim shoulders in the chilly evening.

Charles isn't normally one to stray from his routines. Every day after working at the lab, he walks the same route back to his apartment, showers, fixes himself a microwave dinner, and watches the news. He likes it that way. He's never been interested in spontaneity. But that night at the tavern, he's immediately drawn inside. There's something that pulls him, some subconscious force. And besides that, he likes the atmosphere, the down-to-earth feel.

The bartender offers Charles another drink, and Charles smiles as the bartender fills up his glass. As he takes the mug from the bartender, he notices something, somebody, vaguely reflected. Charles's glasses have again slid down his nose, the lenses foggy with condensation. He takes off the glasses, wipes them on his shirt, and when he puts them back on, Julie stands before him, silent and ethereal.

"Julie?" Surely it can't actually be her.

"Charles!" Julie says, and she wraps Charles in the most enormous hug. She still smells like she always has, like almonds and rose hips and Earl Grey tea. She looks older than the last time Charles saw her. Her face has matured. Then again, Charles imagines he must look older too. He can't even remember the last time they saw each other. Charles thinks about Julie often, but the more he thinks about her, the more unreal she seems, a fairy-tale being in a past that Charles is sure didn't exist. He has picked up the phone so many times, only to put it back down again.

"How did . . . uh . . . what brings you here?" Charles asks. Julie sits down on the stool beside him. A tendril of hair falls in front of her eyes. She pushes it back. She's perfect, so perfect, the way one can be perfect in dreams.

"My uncle owns the tavern. He designed it himself. A nearly identical replica of a French tavern in Provence that's been standing since the seventeen hundreds. His art specializes in the re-creation of history. There's something beautiful in trying to recreate history and admiring the inevitable flaws, don't you think?"

There's a pause as Charles gazes into Julie's eyes. It's as if they've never been apart. As if no time has passed. And yet when Julie puts a hand up to Charles's face, feeling the grooves in his cheekbones, the grizzle along his jaw, Charles is suddenly aware of how old he must look. He has transformed into a tall, solitary man with hardened eyes and a perpetual five o'clock shadow. He's still nice, at certain times and in certain ways, but he's no longer the nice boy who grew up down the street from Julie.

"It's really something," Charles says.

"I would have to agree," Julie says. The bartender brings Julie a drink, something sweet with honey. Julie hands him a basketful of muffins.

"They're from my mother, fresh baked." The bartender smiles and nods and takes the basket behind the counter.

"How did you find your way here?" Julie asks.

"I don't know. I just looked up and here I was."

"How serendipitous."

"Indeed." The air is cold and still between them.

"I haven't seen you in a long time," Julie says quietly.

"I know." Charles looks down. "After I graduated, I just couldn't bring myself to go back to my parents' house. I'm sorry, Julie, you have no idea how sorry I am."

"It's okay," Julie says, taking Charles's hand. Charles holds it for several moments, feeling how perfect it is.

"Are you still living with your mother?" Charles asks.

"Yes, it's the type of place that's difficult to leave. In a good way, of course. The artists are such amazing people, I can't imagine wanting to be surrounded by anybody else. So I help my mother keep up the facilities, run errands. I also have my own studio where I can sculpt and paint. Sometimes I think about leaving, but you know how it is."

"It sounds wonderful," Charles says.

"It can be sometimes. Sometimes not." Julie finishes her drink. "What about you?"

"I'm working at a genetics lab." Charles finishes his drink too and pushes the empty glass next to Julie's. "It's difficult, but I love it. I wouldn't want to be doing anything else."

Julie places a hand on Charles's thigh. Her touch is gentle and light, ghostlike. Charles looks into Julie's eyes, so alive and bright that it's difficult to look away. Before Charles realizes what's happening, he is kissing her. They kiss for a long time before Charles pulls away.

"I've always wanted to do that again," Charles murmurs, still looking into Julie's beautiful eyes, seeing every color in them, green, blue, a fiery orange. "Since the last time we . . . well, I don't know why I never did."

"Because it was meant to happen now," Julie replies, her mouth turned up into a half smile. She slides off the bar stool, pulling Charles along with her. "Come on, let's get out of here. There's somewhere I want to show you."

Charles follows her as she winds her way across the floor and up the stairs. It's raining outside, a slow drizzle, but the air feels warmer as well. Julie doesn't simply walk into the night, she dances, taking care to splash in the puddles and spin through the fat droplets of water pouring off the edge of the roof. Every so often it looks like Julie is about to fall, and Charles swoops forth in his awkward, gangly sort of way to rescue her from danger. They kiss and kiss and kiss again, trying out every different way to do it. Charles can't believe how happy he feels.

The rain falls harder and harder, coming down in sheets. Charles is soaked through to the bone and so is Julie, though the smile never leaves her face. Julie pulls Charles away from the road, through a wooded area in which they must duck under tree branches and jump over logs. Instead of slowing down, Julie's pace grows faster, so that Charles almost has to jog to keep up.

Finally Julie stops. She stands in front of a cave, her mouth slightly ajar with amazement. She pulls Charles forward, a misstep, and she and Charles both tumble face first into the dry cave. Without saying anything, Julie strips Charles of his wet clothing. Charles does the same for her. He pushes the dripping streams of hair out of Julie's face as he kisses her, again and again. Julie's hand explores his warm, soft skin. Their bodies glow in the yellow light of the moon. Finally, when they are both exhausted and content, they curl up in one another's embrace. The rain has stopped and there's a tapestry of stars in the night sky.

"What is this place? There's something about it. Something that doesn't feel quite real," Charles says. Julie lies beside him, her head resting on his arm.

"I know what you mean," Julie says. She takes Charles's chin in her hands and tilts it down for a kiss. Charles wraps Julie up in his arms, pulling her against his chest. Their breathing synchronizes and slows together into something approaching sleep. Just as he's about to nod off, Charles speaks.

"I missed you, Julie."

"I missed you too, Charles."

"Why did we spend so many years apart?"

"I don't know. I don't know. I don't know."

IT'S PAST MIDNIGHT BY THE TIME I TRUDGE UP THE FRONT steps. My pants are soaked and every time I close my eyes, I see Julie plastered on the insides of my eyelids. My senses wish for nothing more than her real person, a person whose skin, whose warmth I can feel against my fingertips, against my chest. It seems inconceivable, that my former self could have been so foolish. Why did we spend so many years apart? So many wasted years.

I flip on the lights to the entryway. The old man is still awake. He sits cross-legged among the marionettes, in an open robe and pinstriped boxers, his big toe sticking out through a hole in his socks. He's moved the oak end table from beside the bed. Lavender sheets hang down from the rafters, creating curtains for a stage. The marionettes have been taken down, and a damp rag beside the old man is dark and musty from scrubbing the dust off their wooden bodies. He takes one of the marionettes in his quavering hand, a young woman with dark hair and hazel eyes, studies the way in which the marionette moves, pulling up and down on the strings, causing her to walk forward and back. He runs his fingers along the grooves of the body, frowning in an unconscious way. He then takes another of the marionettes, a young man with blond hair and blue eyes. He lays them down on the table, side by side, manipulating the young man's arm around the young woman with the strings. The curtain-sheets sway in an imagined wind, and even though we are inside, I can almost see raindrops drizzling down across their faces. The male marionette turns his head.

"I missed you, Julie."

The female marionette tilts her chin up. "I missed you too, Charles."

"Why did we spend so many years apart?"

"I don't know. I don't know. I don't know."

The last line breaks the old man. He chokes on the words. No more will come after that. I lower myself down beside him, unlooping the strings from around his fingers and setting the marionettes aside. I try not to admit to myself how rattled I feel. How does he know the exact words from my memory? Have I recited them to him before? Or is it something less than logical, something beneath a more rational explanation of human consciousness.

"She feels familiar," the old man says. He takes the female marionette, cradling her in his arms, her dark hair spilling over his fingers.

"She looks like Julie."

"But I don't know who that is." His voice is watery, draining away.

That night, I dream of myself in a crisp tuxedo, my hair trimmed, my face freshly shaved. Julie stands beside me, a lacy white wedding dress curving around her body, the cherry red of her lipstick casting a deep, dark imprint as she kisses me on the cheek. We are still, our smiles unchanging, as if we're waiting for our photograph to be taken. Julie places her hand against her abdomen, wincing slightly. I take her in my arms. We continue to wait.

And then, slowly, our smiles wither and fade. We aren't surrounded by our family or our friends or anything at all but a dreary, endless abyss. I reach out my arms, searching the darkness around me, hoping to find something solid, something tangible. As I reach out for Julie, my hands slide through her transparent body, a ghost of a body that no longer exists.

I wake up to the sound of someone knocking at the door. The bedroom is still dark. The sun is just rising, light like egg dripping down the edges of the sky. I stumble out from under the sheets, pull on a pair of jeans and a T-shirt. I walk by and see Einstein and the old man curled up together on the couch, snoring in harmony with one another, marionettes scattered around them. I peer out through the peephole and then open the door. Iris stands on the porch, a mostly asleep Ava draped over her shoulder. Iris's hair is up in a quick bun, dark circles under her eyes.

"I'm sorry to wake you up so early, Charles. Can we come in?"

"Of course, of course. Why don't we go into the other room?" I lead them into the kitchen and Iris takes a seat, maneuvering the sleeping Ava into her lap.

"Coffee?"

"I better not, I can only stay for a minute or two," Iris says.

I put on a kettle of water to boil for myself. Iris strokes Ava's soft red hair, combing through the tangles with her fingers. "Look Charles, I'm sorry about the way I reacted the other day. I shouldn't have—"

"It's okay, I understand. No hard feelings."

"And I'm sorry to have bothered you so early in the morning, especially to ask you for a favor, but I was wondering if you could take Ava for today. My mother-in-law fell down the stairs—she's going to be fine, but she needs someone to go with her to the doctor and she lives in Carlton two hours east from here. And of course Ava doesn't have school today, so . . ."

"I'd be happy to do it." I flash Iris a quick grin. Steam curls out of the kettle.

"Okay. Okay then, well, thank you, Charles. I have to run, but I'll be back tonight, all right?" Iris stands and maneuvers Ava into my arms. Her tiny lungs breathe against mine, her small, wet mouth soaking into my shoulder. As soon as Iris shuts the front door, Ava's eyes pop wide open. I wonder if she was faking sleep the whole time.

"Can we have French toast for breakfast?" she asks. She reaches up her hand and brushes it against my cheek. "You need to shave."

"Yes, I need to shave, and yes, we can have French toast for breakfast. You want to help?"

Ava nods and I set her up on the countertop. I crack a few eggs into a metal bowl, then hand her the whisk. "You know how to do this?"

"Course I do."

I pour myself a cup of coffee and then start a pan sizzling with butter. I take out a loaf of bread and some milk. I watch Ava's concentration, biting her lower lip as she whisks the eggs, determined to make them uniform. Einstein trots into the room and licks up the bit of egg that Ava drips onto the floor. I wonder if I used to make breakfast with Jess, if she was as serious a whisker as Ava.

"What are we gonna do today?"

"How do you feel about coming with me to work?" I say, dipping the bread into the egg mixture.

"Is there gonna be stuff to play with?"

"Of course, lots and lots of stuff."

"Are you like Dr. Frankenstein?" My mind flashes to the memory of the woman and the young girl, deformed and twisting, moaning in pain.

"Why do you ask that, Ava?"

"I dunno. He was really cool. If I were a scientist, I would make a monster and I would name him Rory and we would hang out all the time together."

I don't know what to say to this, so instead I finish cooking the French toast and set a plate at the table for Ava. I scoop her up like a paper doll and set her down. "Better eat up before it gets cold." Ava pours a swimming pool of syrup over the French toast and chows down. I fry up my own batch.

"When's my mom coming back?" Ava says through a mouthful.

"Tonight. She should be coming back tonight."

Ava takes a big gulp of orange juice. "Did you have a mom?"

"I did."

"Is she still alive?"

"No, she's not."

"Did you love her?"

"Yes, very much." I sit down across from Ava. Einstein hops into my lap and starts purring. The French toast is good but a bit overdone.

"And you had a dad too?" Ava asks after a moment.

"Yes."

"But he's dead, right?"

"Yes, he is."

"Did you love him?"

I look down at my plate of soggy French toast. I'm at a loss for words.

"Of course I did. Everyone loves their parents," I finally say.

June 13, 1982

Age Four

Charles sits in a waiting room. His feet don't touch the floor and he swings his legs back and forth. He pushes his glasses up his nose, squirms in the uncomfortable clothing his mother made him wear. The shirt scratches at the back of his neck, and the khaki pants are too small for him. His mother sits in the armchair beside him. She too is well dressed, wearing a long navy dress with buttons down the front, red lipstick, and a black velvet box hat with several curls peeking out from underneath. She crosses her legs, opens a Time *magazine. The cover article is about Steve Jobs and Apple computers, the headline: "Striking it Rich: America's Risk Takers." Beethoven plays on a record behind them, an antique clock ticking on the reception desk. The wallpaper is stuffy and dull, and the waiting room smells like paper and cologne.*

The receptionist looks down at a clipboard. "Dr. Hebson will see you now," the receptionist announces. Charles checks around the room. He and his mother are the only two people there. His mother takes his hand and leads him down the hallway.

"Now remember," she says. "You aren't to tell your father about any of this."

Charles nods as they enter a sparsely decorated office. There's a houseplant, a bookshelf, a desk, and a couch. The couch is blue, nondescript. A man rises from behind the desk, adjusts his tie, and straightens his jacket. He reaches his hand out to Charles's mother. She shakes it and then she and Charles sit down on the couch. She keeps her hand on Charles's knee the whole time, unusual for her. Not the touch. She always tries to be warm and loving to Charles, but her grip seems nervous, as if she's holding onto the knee to anchor herself. Charles attempts to slide his knee away.

"So what brings you here today?" the man asks. He takes out a black leather binder from one of the drawers and jots several notes. The man is muscular and broad-shouldered, with the sort of jocular smile that puts people at ease. He's the man from the funeral, the one who was holding a photograph of Charles's mother.

"I'm concerned about Charles," she says, nodding her head toward him. He doesn't look up, instead counting something on his fingers.

"What particularly are you concerned about?"

Charles's mother lowers her voice. "He seems different from the other children. He's in his own world. He prefers playing alone and he'll become engrossed, almost obsessed with the mechanics of whatever interests him at a particular time. I'm just worried and I've heard . . "

"I see," the man says.

"I just want to make sure, if there is something wrong—"

"Why don't you leave Charles with me for the next half hour or so and I'll ask some questions, maybe do a few tests. You're wel-

come to sit in the waiting room. Help yourself to some coffee or tea."

"Thank you, Dr. Hebson." She plants a kiss on Charles's forehead before she leaves the room.

"Everything's going to be just fine," he assures her.

A half hour later, the man emerges from the office with Charles. Charles holds open an issue of National Geographic, *absorbed in an article about emus. He has a wide grin on his face as the man pats the top of his head and gestures to his mother. She springs up from her seat, clasps her hands together as she walks toward the man.*

"Well?" she asks. "What do you think?"

"He's fine," the man replies. "Nothing to be concerned about. He's very smart, you know."

"Yes, I'm quite aware," she says. In the meantime, Charles continues thumbing through the National Geographic.

"He's just very logical. Terrific problem-solving skills."

"But there's nothing wrong?"

The man gives the mother an earnest look. "Do you want something to be wrong?"

Charles's mother shakes her head and again lowers her voice. "Of course not. I just . . . I don't think he loves me."

"I'm sure that he does," the man says, and then he leans in and whispers into her ear. "I don't think that's what this is really about."

Charles's mother steps back, putting her hand up to her left eye, feeling the purple swelling she tried to hide with makeup.

"It was an accident," she says. "My husband had an accident." She goes to lead Charles out of the waiting room. The man takes her arm.

"I can help you, you know. If you let me, I can help you."

"I'm just fine, thank you." She tugs Charles out the door, but just before slamming it behind her, she sneaks a glance back at Dr. Hebson.

I STEP OUTSIDE INTO THE CRISP MORNING AIR WITH AVA in one arm and several pillows in the other. Iris didn't mention anything about a car seat, but I'm pretty sure that Ava is too small not to have one. I pack her in between the pillows.

"We're playing pillow fort," I explain to her as she wiggles against the seat belt.

"Then how come you don't have a pillow fort?" she protests.

"Because I'm the pillow fort driver. Every pillow fort needs a driver."

I'm hoping that I still know how to drive. I haven't tried since I first arrived back at the house. But the car in the driveway seems sturdy enough, a rust-red Subaru wagon from the early 1990s. I feel the muscle memory return as soon as I put my keys in the ignition and disable the emergency brake. It's freeing to realize that if I really wanted, I could just keep driving. I could drive far, far away.

On the way to work, Ava mostly hums to herself, the same tune, over and over.

"What are you humming?"

"It's from *Peter Pan*. It's called 'I Won't Grow Up.' It was my favorite song last year."

"Why was it your favorite song last year?"

"Because my school did the musical *Peter Pan* and I got to play a fairy."

I think about Jess, swooping around the living room with her friends. "You know, my daughter, Jess, always loved being a fairy too."

Ava pulls something out from under her. One of the marionettes. A young girl, her face shining, her hair swept back into a ponytail, a princess dress swirling around her feet.

"Is this what Jess used to look like?" Ava asks.

"Yes," I say. "At least, that's how I remember her." At the next red light, I turn back to her. "Ava, I have a question. Am I much different now?"

"Different from when?"

"You know, before I left."

Ava pauses, chewing on her lower lip. "Kinda, I guess. You were sad a lot. You didn't want me to know but I could tell. Sometimes when you told a joke that was supposed to be funny, it made me sad instead."

"And I seem happier now?"

"You're smiling more. I like that."

I pull into the underground parking structure and gather Ava in my arms. We navigate through the maze of cars and concrete columns before taking the elevator up to the fifth floor. She insists on making rocket ship sounds the entire way up.

"Do you ever feel scared?" she asks.

"Scared of what?"

"The ghost."

The elevator pings. "The ghost? What ghost?"

"The ghost who lives at your house," she says matter-of-factly.

It takes me a moment. "You mean the old man?"

Ava nods her head. I shift her to my back as we walk down the hallway. Her legs cling around my waist like a marsupial.

"I don't think he's a ghost."

"Are you sure?"

"Pretty sure."

"Then who is he?"

"He's a relative, I think."

"Because he seems haunted. Have you seen how he just like floats around?"

I can tell that I'm unlikely to win this battle. Besides, I'm not entirely convinced Ava's wrong. I don't know what to believe in anymore. "Well, even if he's a ghost, there's no reason to be scared. He has a good heart."

"How do you know?"

"I just know."

"But how?"

I put my keycard up to the sensor and the door whizzes open. Scientists bustle through the main lobby, clipboards in one hand, coffee in the other, murmuring under their breath about data sets and confounding variables. The faces are anonymous. Nobody stops to say hello.

I turn down the corridor and around the corner. The last door on the right is marked in bold block letters across the frosted glass—HUMAN RESOURCES. Classical music emanates out, something familiar and bright, Tchaikovsky perhaps. I give a light knock.

"Come in," a feminine voice trills from inside, and I push open the door. A middle-aged woman sits typing on her computer. Her blond hair is folded into a glossy updo. A bookshelf holds a dusty, leather-bound set of encyclopedias that I would guess to be at least one hundred years old. Otherwise the office is entirely modern, ergonomic chairs and the latest touch screen devices.

"May I help you?"

"Um, yes, I'm Charles, Charles Lang? Peter said to stop by HR to pick up some paperwork."

The woman doesn't respond, instead diving into a filing cabinet beneath her desk. She emerges with a manila envelope marked with my name.

"Make sure to get your paperwork completed and signed by the end of the week," she says, handing me the envelope. She then checks the Post-its lining the edge of her computer monitor. She plucks one from the right corner.

"Also," she continues, "you have an appointment with Katherine DeFazio on the first floor"—she checks her watch —"five minutes ago. You better get going. She's in room 106."

"I'm sorry, who's Katherine DeFazio?"

"I don't know. I'm just the messenger." The woman returns to her typing.

I enter the adjacent stairwell and trample down the steps. Who's Katherine DeFazio and why didn't Peter tell me about our meeting yesterday? I wonder if she's a client of ours, if she's expecting me to have something prepared. I lick my lips over and over again, my mouth arid. Ava shares in none of my anxieties, instead giggling and pulling on my hair as if I'm some sort of carnival ride. Ava—I didn't consider how inappropriate it might be for me to bring a small child to a meeting. I suppose it's too late to do anything about that.

Room 106. *Katherine DeFazio, MFT.* I pause for a moment. The black letters look crooked. There's an amateurish quality to them. They look like they've been spray-painted onto the door with a stencil.

"Mr. Lang?" A young woman pokes her head out of the room. She's beautiful, her dark, straight hair cropped short in a bob. She wears a warm shade of red lipstick that makes her seem mature, although she's at least several years younger than me. She has thin, fine eyebrows reminiscent of a doll's, the kind of wide eyes preteens reserve for celebrities.

"Um, yes, yes, that's me. Charles, you can call me Charles."

"Katie. Katie DeFazio," the young woman says, sticking out her hand. "Why don't you come inside?"

I shake Katie's hand and follow her into the room, shifting Ava up onto my shoulders. The office is not what I expected. The sharp fluorescence of the lab has been replaced by the glow of flickering candles. A violet hydrangea sits on a coffee table next to a box of tissues. Several watercolor paintings hang on the walls, depicting meandering sunsets, flowers blooming in springtime, and a sailboat drifting away at sea. I sit down on one of the couches as the woman lowers herself into a black leather chair across from me. Ava wriggles down onto the rug, playing with the marionette of the girl.

"Sorry, I didn't—"

"Don't worry, I love children." Katie takes a folder out of the desk and opens it on her lap. I notice she keeps sneaking glances at me. I shift my gaze downward, studying the backs of my hands.

"Katie, would you mind telling me what we're meeting about?"

Katie's cheeks flush bright red. "You mean, Peter didn't tell you?"

"I can't say that he did."

"Well then." For a moment, it almost seems like she's rehearsing something under her breath. "Well, we're going to be meeting over the next several weeks, to see how you're feeling. How you're adjusting."

"Like a therapist?"

"You could say that. Sorry for the surprise. Peter mentioned that it was a condition of your resumed employment?"

"I suppose that makes sense." I look up. Katie smiles, an earnest smile. I don't know if it's real or not. She looks even younger sitting down, like she's barely out of college.

"Would you mind telling me what's in the file?" I ask. "Not every single detail, just, you know, any main points. If that's okay."

"Of course." Katie opens the file, skims through it.

"Well, there's not much, hmm, all right, two and a half years ago, patient reported the disappearance of his wife, Julie, and daughter, Jess . . . continued with position at the lab but coworkers reported observing increasingly manic and depressive behaviors . . . psychiatric evaluation inconclusive but suggestive of posttraumatic stress disorder . . . January 31, 2010, psychotic episode while at the lab . . . and then nothing has been recorded since then . . . is this difficult to hear?"

"No, it's helpful, actually. Sort of. Peter mentioned that I had an aneurysm six months ago?"

"Right. Peter did say something about that."

We sit in silence. Ava manipulates the marionette onto the coffee table.

"So how are you, Charles? How are you feeling today?"

"I . . . I—" The room swirls and fades around me.

November 14, 2004

Age Twenty-Six

Julie sits on the floor of the living room, her legs splayed out to one side. Her hair coils down her back, dragging across the ground, like a snake in waiting. Charles squats down beside her, frowning slightly. He's still in his slacks and a dress shirt from work. Towers of cardboard moving boxes surround them as well as an entire militia of marionettes. Julie hums to herself as she helps the marionettes to their feet, allowing them to interact with one another. Charles touches Julie's arm.

"What's wrong?" Julie says without looking up. She adjusts the shirt collar on one of the marionettes, sewing a rip.

"The baby was crying, you know. Just now. I fed her and rocked her to sleep. Did you even hear her?"

"I was distracted. I'm sorry."

"You spend all day with those marionettes. I'm beginning to worry."

"Trust me, Charles. It'll all come together."

"Julie."

"They were a gift from my mother." Julie clutches the marionette to her chest, her eyes wide like a scared child. She looks fragile enough to break into a million little pieces. "You don't like them, do you?"

Charles turns so that he's facing Julie. He does his best to soften his tone. "It's not that. I just don't understand why they're so important to you."

"You wouldn't believe me if I told you why."

"Try me."

"Well, they have answers. They exert influence, and if you ask them the right questions, if you can learn to understand their language . . ."

"Answers? Like what sorts of answers?"

"They're predictive, in a way. If you know the questions to ask, the way to feel the answers."

"What do you mean?"

"How do you think we came to bump into each other that night at the tavern? How do you think I knew when to be there?"

"It was coincidence. Chance. Luck."

"It was meant to be. It was a story my mother had told me over and over again, when I was little. I just hadn't realized what it meant at the time."

"Julie, you can't honestly believe in all that, can you?"

Tears well up in Julie's eyes, her eyelids quavering in the face of a flood. She hadn't always been this delicate. She had been stronger, fierce even, but since they had reconnected, since they had had Jess, there was just something intangibly different about Julie, something fleeting.

Charles rises, folding his arms across his chest. He remembers a dream he had the night they slept together in the cave, a dream he had decided not to tell Julie in the morning. The dream had involved an image of himself, his dream self, sleeping side by side in the cave with Julie. Except that in the dream, he had awakened in the middle of the night to a strange burning sensation in his hands and feet. He had looked down to discover that extending from his wrists and knees were two sets of long, woven strings continuing out of the cave, through the stars, and past the moon to a wooden cross in the middle of the universe. Every once in a while the strings would pull up or down, causing his arms and legs to move. The next morning, as he'd pulled on his damp, dusty clothes, Charles had told himself that it was just a dream. He repeated this again and again, not wanting to admit to himself that a part of him was sure the dream was real.

"I'm sorry. I'm sorry I overreacted," Charles finally says. He sits down again on the floor, taking Julie's wet face in his hands and kissing her forehead. She crumples against him, lighter, less solid than she should be. "But if you're right, what does that mean? That we have no free will? That everything is fated?" Julie doesn't answer. "What about my parents? Were they just destined to die?"

Julie wipes her nose and kisses the back of Charles's neck, underneath the tuft of hair in the area she calls his kiss garden. There's something ghostly about the way her lips graze his flesh. "It's just a way of getting information. Isn't that what scientists spend their entire lives doing? Looking for ways to read the world? This is just the way my family learned to do it. My grandmother taught my mother and my mother taught me."

"And what if the marionettes tell you something you don't want

to know? What then?" The night is too dark. The air is too still.

"I don't ask questions like that," Julie murmurs. Her voice grows fainter. Charles reaches to take hold of her as she dissolves away into the nighttime.

"Charles, how are you feeling?" Katie asks the question again. Ava continues to play with the marionette. I look up at a clock across the room. The second hand ticks by. It feels like hours have gone by, but no time has passed. The rest of the session remains uneventful, and after we finish, I hardly remember what we've discussed.

I take the elevator back upstairs and slide my keycard into the slot. Ava hangs down around my shoulders, her small fingers sunk into the grooves of my shirt collar. The doors open and I step inside the lobby, empty except for a dark-haired man in a lab coat. He whistles to himself behind the counter in the kitchenette. He stirs his coffee in time with the whistling, using the disposable wooden stick to conduct. For a moment, I'm sure I'm hallucinating, or maybe still in a memory.

"Steve?"

The man glances up, startled. "Charles? Is that you?"

Steve looks practically the same as he did in high school, the same nest of black curls, the same round spectacles and flushed cheeks, except that he's taller, slimmer, a slight hunch to his shoulders, wrinkles skirting across his forehead. He sets down his cup of coffee.

"Uncle Steve!" Ava squeals. She swings down as if dismounting from the jungle gym on a playground.

"May I?" Steve asks. I nod. He scoops her into the air, swirling her around and around, enveloped by a chorus of giggles that seem like they're coming from more than one little girl.

"No more! No more!" she finally gasps, and Steve sets Ava down, plopping a big kiss on her head.

"Now you go run around, honeybunch, and don't get into any trouble."

As Ava streaks down the corridor, Steve turns to me. There's a strange look in his eyes, something indiscernible, almost like excitement and sadness and apprehension all mixed into one.

"I take it you two know each other?"

"You used to bring her around quite a bit. I've missed her. She's grown so much in the past six months."

I pause. "And I imagine we've been working together for a while as well?"

Steve nods. "About three years. Give or take a few months."

"Am I okay, Steve? Am I going to be okay?"

"Of course, Charles. Your memory will come back. You're going to be fine."

"Can I ask you—"

"Yes, of course."

"How did it come about? The two of us working together? All I can remember is being kids and then you running away . . ."

Steve takes off his glasses. He massages the ridge of his nose. "I know. I wish I'd done things differently, but it was all I could think to do at the time."

"Where were you? Julie and I couldn't believe you'd just left us."

Steve turns to watch Ava for a moment. She loops back toward us, chattering away to the marionette. "I bummed around Europe for a while, Poland and Hungary and the Czech Republic, crashed on couches or in the street, did odd jobs for folks. Eventually I saved up enough money to get to London, applied to school, got a scholarship. I studied bioengineering, met Richard. We decided to move back to the States. I called you when I got back. I thought you would hate me. I was kind of afraid you wouldn't even remember me. I know that sounds crazy but it had been over ten years since we'd last talked. You were kind, though. Empathetic. You got me an interview with Genutech."

"What did I say? Did I tell you about anything that had happened since you left?"

"A little. Not much. I really had to pull it out of you. You told me that your parents had died, that you were living in their old house. That you had married Julie. That you had a daughter named Jess."

"Did you meet her? Did you get to meet Jess? What was Julie like then?"

"I don't know. I didn't get to see either of them when I moved back, before they . . ." Steve frowns. "Well, I kept suggesting we all get together but it never quite worked out, and then a few months later . . . I think you were too nice to say it, but I'm pretty sure Julie wanted nothing to do with me. Which I get. Ultimately it was my fault. I just took off. It was a selfish thing to do." Steve checks his watch. "Sorry,

Charles, I have a meeting to get to, but I'm glad you're back."

"Steve?"

"Mmm?"

"Do I seem different to you?"

Steve's smile sinks, his words anchored down. "I have to go, Charles. I'll see you soon."

Before I can say anything else, Steve has already disappeared, leaving behind nothing but the discarded stirrer from his coffee. Ava abandons the marionette, bored, and tugs on my sleeve. "Can we go see the jellyfish?"

"Sure thing. It's about time I updated my notes."

Ava claps her hands together, grinning as I unlock the door to my room at the lab. The blinds are open on the windows above the tanks and shades of orange and pink smear across the wall in the early morning light. Ava presses her face up to the glass, mesmerized by the luminous bodies of the jellyfish, the way they swoop around each another, their tentacles reacting warmly to one another's touch.

"They seem so peaceful. They're like angels," Ava whispers, as if talking any louder will disturb the jellyfish. I can see what she means, the way the jellyfish just sway from side to side with every vibration of the water. I make my rounds, recording the progress of my experiments, examining marine samples in petri dishes under the microscope, thinking about how grateful I am that the memory loss left my scientific knowledge unharmed. The tanks are so tall that I have to stand on a footstool to reach into each one, rubber glove up to my right elbow, taking each jellyfish into my hand so that I can inspect it more closely and describe any changes in coloration, size, or behavior. Several of the tanks hold the jellyfish that are part of the control group, while others have been exposed to various chemical catalysts. About two-thirds of the tanks appear empty, but in reality, each contains a tiny sample of undifferentiated cells in a miniature incubation chamber at the bottom. I make my way around the room until I reach the last tank, my eyes fastened to my clipboard, searching for patterns.

I almost don't notice it, distracted by the numbers and figures already written down, but just as I'm about to step down from the footstool, I see a slight glint out of the corner of my eye. Inside the incubation chamber is a tiny, iridescent jellyfish, shimmering silver and purple in the water. I blink once, twice, wanting to make sure I'm not imagining it, that I don't have something in my eye. But no, the truth is that from just a few transdifferentiated cells, I've created a life.

January 29, 2004

Age Twenty-Six

Julie asks Charles to meet her in the park. The day feels like January, the air clear and crisp, slightly wet. Charles pulls his scarf more tightly around his neck, checks to make sure the rose is still safely stowed in his breast pocket. Charles finally spots Julie standing beneath a broad oak tree, her cheeks pink with the cold. He jogs up to her and wraps his arms around her, pecking her on the lips. Charles takes out the rose and hands it to Julie.

"What's this for?" Julie says.

"I know it's probably silly, but it's been exactly a month since we saw each other at the tavern, and I just wanted to give you a little something," Charles says.

"The color is . . . well, it's brilliant. I've never seen a color quite like it." The rose is somewhere between deep violet and blue, a color that seems to shift in the sunlight. Julie smiles and tucks the rose into her bag. She takes Charles's hand and leads him to a bench to sit down.

"Charles, there's something I need to tell you."

"Is something wrong?"

"I—I'm pregnant," Julie says. For several moments, it feels like time freezes. The wind grows still, the birds perching silently, the woman by the drinking fountain pausing midstep. Charles holds Julie in his arms, brings her close into his chest so that her head is burrowed into his shoulder. Julie looks up at Charles and when their eyes meet, they both grin.

"We're going to have a baby," Charles says, barely able to contain his excitement.

"Yes, we are!" Julie starts to laugh. "I was so scared to tell you. I don't know why. I thought maybe you would freak out or be angry or something."

Charles takes Julie's chin in his hand and kisses her. "I love you, Julie. I want to marry you. I want to have children with you. I want to spend the rest of my life with you, and the fact that we've created something beautiful together is just, it's spectacular."

Julie squeezes Charles's hand. "I feel the same way."

"So that's that," Charles says.

"That's that," Julie says. "Except—"

"Except?"

"Well, there was something else I wanted to talk to you about. My room is so cramped, your apartment is so small . . . we should clean out your parents' house, Charles. It's just going to waste right now and if we're going to have a family together, we're going to need space. Not to mention how nice it would be to still live so close to my mother."

"Oh."

"Oh?"

"I just, I don't know. I don't know." Charles stands up. He feels his chest closing in.

"Charles, I can be patient. We can take it really slow. We have time to figure this out," Julie says. "Come on, sit down. Take a deep breath."

Charles lets Julie guide him back down to the bench. He breathes in and out, trying to push away the panicked feeling.

"I haven't been back since the funeral," Charles admits. "I don't know if I can."

"You're going to have to face it eventually, though," Julie says quietly.

"I know it doesn't seem rational. But the last time I went, it just felt like the house was toxic, like every object, every photo, every piece of furniture triggered some sort of terrible memory. I told myself I never wanted to feel like that again."

"I understand, Charles. You have to trust me on this."

Charles hangs his head. "I don't know. I don't know if I can."

"You know, everyone assumes that my mother has always been alone, that she was never married, that my father was never

around," Julie says. "They don't know that my parents were happy together, that my father had cancer and died when I was five. I started having panic attacks right around the time he died. I had no idea what they were at first. I was convinced I was dying too. I would have stomachaches and headaches, and it felt like my chest was caving in on itself. At a certain point, my mother figured out that they were always triggered by the objects I associated with my father—his old razor sitting on the bathroom counter, his pants hanging in the closet, his paintings on the living room walls."

"I'm sorry, I didn't know. I don't know how I didn't—"

"Because I didn't tell you. I don't tell anybody."

"I'm sorry," Charles says again. Then, "What was his name?"

"Rolf. He was half German, half British, with long, lanky limbs and hair blonder than anybody else I'd ever seen before."

Charles takes Julie's hand in his. He gives it a warm squeeze. "And what was he like?"

"My mother says he was quiet and contemplative, an honest person. He didn't know any other way to be but genuine. He was a painter. He would paint in our living room, just in his jeans. He liked to work with his shirt off. He liked the feeling of getting splattered with paint and having to scrub it off in the shower at night. I thought he was invincible. He was the tallest, strongest man I knew."

"What else do you remember?"

"He always read to me at night, and my favorite book was an old, worn copy of Peter Pan. *At that time, my greatest fear was that I wouldn't be able to be a child forever. One day my father took me in his lap and said he had a secret to tell me, a secret I must not tell anybody else. He told me that even if he looked like a grown-up, he was really a child at heart, and that these sorts of*

things tended to run in families so I really had nothing to worry about. And I believed him. I used to believe that."

"Do you miss him? Uh, sorry, that's a dumb question. Of course you do."

"I think about what my life would've been like if he were around. My mother started hosting the artists' colony at our house the year after he died. She couldn't stand to be alone so she tried to surround herself with as many people as possible. And I loved the company, really, I did. It's just that sometimes I wished I could have been enough for her."

"I know the feeling," Charles says. The wind has struck up again but the sun feels warm against his face.

"What about you?" Julie says. "Do you miss your parents?"

"I have nightmares about them all the time. I'll have the same one over and over again, or at least the same type. I find out, after the funeral, that they're still alive. But they're injured or ill, and I know that they're going to die again soon. And I don't know what to do. I don't know what to tell people. I just don't."

Julie scoots in closer to Charles. He pulls his thick wool coat around her to block out the wind. Julie takes Charles's hand and guides it to her abdomen. He places his gloved fingers against the cotton of her shirt. She puts her hand on top of his.

"Julie, sometimes I think I don't remember everything from the accident. That there's something important, something I blocked out."

"Forever is composed of nows," she says. "Nothing is going to replace your loss. But love and life and fate have enabled us to create a life together. There's something extraordinary in that, something miraculous. All you need to remember is that."

"I MEAN, IT'S CRAZY, I KEEP SEEING THAT SMALL, translucent jellyfish, floating around the tank, fully formed, fully functioning, one hundred percent alive. And I can't help thinking—I've done it! I've unlocked the secret, the process by which all adult cells can be transformed into stem cells and then cultivated to become whatever we'd like. The implications are just extraordinary. We could create new tissue from small samples of existing human cells. Patients would no longer have to waste away waiting on transplant lists—they would be able to use their own tissue to grow new, healthy organs using three-dimensional printing. And that's only the beginning. I could revolutionize the potential of cloning, and if my hunch is correct, the boundaries of life and death themselves. Because this jellyfish that I created—it's not just a heart or an eye or a tentacle. I was able to combine the tissues in such a way that they are able to function together as an entirely new, viable life. This is a step beyond Dolly, beyond the embryonic cloning practices of the past. Using just a few cells with intact DNA, I can replicate an organism so that the copy is at the same level of physical and mental maturity as its original predecessor. Don't you see? The myths of science fiction are becoming a reality. A four-year-old jellyfish would spawn a clone that was four years old as well. And perhaps someday a forty-year-old human could do the same."

I pause to catch my breath, gulping down a glass of tap water from the countertop. I'm in Iris's kitchen, pacing back and forth as she places a chocolate Bundt cake into the oven. My hair's sticking up in sweaty tufts, and I can feel my cheeks glowing hot and red under the kitchen lights. Iris gazes up at me, biting her lower lip. She has a concerned expression on her face, as a mother might for a delusional child.

"Charles, are you sure you don't want to sit down?"

"I can't, because, you know, here's the thing—since the genome was first discovered, scientists have wondered why it is that some sequences of DNA code for the production of proteins that are absolutely vital to keeping the body alive, while other sequences of DNA seem to have no function, to be entire wastelands of unutilized adenine, guanine, cytosine, and thymine. But as it turns out, this isn't the case. While I'm not yet sure of the mechanism by which it happens, my observations have indicated that these sites are actually repositories for memory. Somehow our memories get transcribed on these sequences, meaning if an organism were replicated, the copy would be physically identical but could also potentially have the same memories as the original. Which, if perfected in human beings, would mean that cloning could enable a person's deceased loved ones to come back to life. Not literally, of course, it wouldn't be the exact originals, but maybe these clones, these replacements could yield people just as good."

Iris sets the timer on the oven and then comes over to me, placing her hand on my wrist. "Charles, please, sit down." She leads me to the dining room table and takes a seat across from me. Ava coos and cackles from the other room, engrossed in her own imagined universe.

"Look, I know what I'm saying might sound crazy, but trust me, it isn't. This could end up being one of the greatest discoveries of the twenty-first century . . . what is it? Why are you looking at me like that?"

Iris frowns. "Charles, it's just—this isn't the first time you've said things like this."

"What do you mean, 'things like this'?"

"I mean, these exact 'discoveries,' Charles. About the cells and the new tissues. How the DNA sequences somehow have our memories in them. How we could clone people and bring them back to life."

"What are you talking about?"

"About six months, just before you disappeared or went away or whatever happened, I don't remember every single word you said, but I swear, you came in one night and you were saying almost exactly the same things you're saying now. And after that, you started becoming more distant. Ava and I hardly saw you anymore."

"Oh." There's a sinking feeling in my stomach, a heaviness right at the base of my ribcage. "Well, I guess the news isn't as exciting as I thought."

Iris turns to me. "Be excited, Charles. Be as excited as you want. But be careful. I don't want to lose you again."

I DON'T GET HOME UNTIL JUST BEFORE MIDNIGHT. THE wind whips through the trees, possessed, the phone wires crackling in response. I shut the door quietly and peel off my jacket, not wanting to disturb the old man, wherever he may be sleeping. I try to be careful, but a moment later, my foot catches on a dining room chair that's been left in the entry-way. I stumble forward and almost fall face first. The chair thuds against the hardwood floor. I wonder why there's a chair in the middle of the room. I flip the light switch by the living room and then jump back with a start. The old man has been sitting in the entryway this entire time, his back straight like a plank against the wall, gazing catatonically into the distance. He doesn't move as I approach him, although I can tell by the gentle rise and fall of his chest that he's not dead. I notice a line of red rope burn around his neck. The skin is rubbed almost raw in some places. I look up and see several of the marionette strings hanging in a loop in the rafters above.

The old man suddenly opens his eyes, thick black pupils looking up at me.

"Talk to me," I say. "How can I help you if I don't even know who you are?"

He remains silent.

"I know what you tried to do," I continue. "Please, just talk to me."

The old man pauses. He licks his crusty lips. There's some sort of white dust settled on his shoulders, like paint or crumbled drywall. "They were staring at me. The marionettes. I just couldn't stand them staring at me anymore."

"Then we should get rid of them. They're not doing either of us any good."

The old man shakes his head no.

"Is it because they were Julie's?" I ask him.

"They have the answers," he says, speaking to nobody. "I know they do. I just need to figure out the right questions."

PART III

The weeks pass by unintentionally, rapidly but without substance, like a film montage. My conversations at work feel artificial, rehearsed, and after my strange encounter with Iris, I wonder if everything I'm doing now is just recycled material. But then why wouldn't Peter say something? Why wouldn't he tell me that I'm conducting research I've already done, that I'm making discoveries I've already made? I want to trust Steve, to imagine that he's on my side, but all I've been able to get out of him is small talk. We talk about the weather, about petri dishes and multiplying cells, about mundane weekend plans involving sleeping in and grocery shopping. Whenever I try to draw out information from him about the past, like someone so delicately trying to extricate a single thread from a piece of fabric, he closes down and walks away, claiming to be busy with some sort of experiment.

In fact, the only person I feel like I can be honest with is Katie. There's an innocence to her demeanor, a sense of genuineness, and I get the feeling that she truly cares about what I have to say. Every time I see her, my heart gives a slight twinge, and I realize that there's something of Julie in her, that I see shadows of my wife in her smile, her gestures.

One morning I knock on the door to Katie's office for our appointment. Silence. I try knocking again. Usually she opens the door before I even knock, as if she has some intuitive knowledge of my presence. But today she's five, ten, fifteen minutes late. I pace back and forth, fiddling with a paperclip in my lab coat pocket. Finally I twist the knob. The door is unlocked.

"Hello?" I call out as I enter. I don't want to disturb Katie's privacy. I expect the office to be empty, or for Katie to be listening to music on her iPod, nodding her head, having lost track of time. Instead, I discover her sitting at her desk, biting her nails. The overhead lights are off and the curtains are drawn.

Katie looks like an apparition of her former self. Her face is empty of color, her mascara smudged around her eyes. Her sweater is unevenly buttoned and her hair is flat and drab against her ears. The room has been torn apart, all of the degrees pulled off the walls, all the potted plants turned over. Katie looks up at me bewildered.

"Charles . . ."

"It's ten o'clock."

"I know," Katie replies vacantly.

"What's wrong?"

Katie doesn't say anything. I make my way toward the desk. Katie slumps in her chair. I crouch down, and very gently, I wrap my arms around Katie. Her eyes dart back and forth, and then she leans in close to me, her lips against my ear.

"Charles, I'm not who you think I am," she whispers, so quietly I can barely hear.

I open my mouth to speak. She puts her hand up over my face, like she's afraid someone might read my lips. "What are you talking about?"

Katie lets out a deep breath, takes another one in. "I'm not a therapist," she says, still in a whisper.

"What?"

"I'm not a therapist. I didn't study psychology. I'm a research assistant."

"A research assistant? For who? What do you mean?"

"Peter hired me. To observe you. To study you."

I sit down on the carpet, shaking my head. "Peter? Why would he want to do that?"

"I don't know. I don't know why, he didn't tell me anything more than he thought I needed to know. He said it was for research, for his research. I don't know what that means."

"Research? Research on what? On me?"

"I don't know." She massages her temples. "I'm just a college student. There was a flier on the bulletin board in the Bio Department. And when I heard that you were going to be involved, that I would get to work one-on-one with such a famous scientist . . ."

"A college student? Look, Katie, what exactly did Peter tell you? What did he want?"

"I was supposed to pretend to be a psychologist. He was interested in your memory. He has hidden video cameras set up around the room. I tried to disable them all, but I'm not sure . . . well, I'm done. I'm out." She looks up at me with a mournful expression. "He has your lab rigged too. One of the jellyfish tanks has a one-way mirror. I don't know which. And

I'm pretty sure your house as well . . . I'm sorry, I shouldn't have ever—he promised me a job at a major research institution when I finished. He said he had connections at Stanford and Harvard."

"What about the degrees on the walls?"

"It was all fake, Charles. All of it."

I pull Katie closer, my lips against her ear. "Why are you telling me all of this? Why now?"

"Because I like you. And because I'm starting to get the feeling that I'm in over my head." She packs up the last of her belongings into her purse.

"Please, if there's anything else—"

"I'm sorry, I have to go." And with that, Katie is out the door before I can say another word. I try to follow her, I push myself forward, but my head is spinning, a kaleidoscope of colors and images whirling before me.

June 13, 2006

Age Twenty-Eight

Charles arrives at the beige building an hour early. He checks his watch, paces back and forth. His shirt is freshly ironed, his slim tie hanging just below his navel. He knows that it's perhaps inappropriate to have shown up this early for his first day of work, but he can't help himself. He's excited, ecstatic. He can't believe he's been given such an amazing opportunity. Charles has spent the past six years ricocheting between research positions—nonprofit start-ups that have gone instantly broke, university labs corrupted by campus politics, biomedical giants overrun by bureaucracy and ethical corruption. But this could be it. He feels it throughout his body. This could be the beginning of the rest of his career.

It's a small lab called Genutech staffed by only a dozen scientists, funded by a group of highly wealthy investors committed to supporting the most cutting-edge biogenetic research. The philosophical ideology behind the company is that autonomy and purpose are the cornerstones of innovation, innovation that will benefit both society as a whole and the investors. Employees are thus given total free reign over their own projects, with the only stipulations being that they present their findings every two months and that each project is pursued with the underlying intent of giving back to the community and/or improving conditions for humankind. Moreover, the chief researcher at the lab is Peter Schiff, a kingpin in the field of biotechnology. Charles can't imagine a more perfect way to provide for his family, for Julie and Jess, Julie who has spoken about having another child and Jess who is about to start preschool.

Charles attempts to delay his arrival—he feigns interest in a newspaper left in the lobby, goes to the bathroom, takes a long swig from the drinking fountain—but after fifteen minutes or so, he can't help but take the elevator up to the lab. He tries his keycard once and then twice. The magnetic strip seems to have no effect. Just as he's about to attempt it a third time, somebody opens the door, a short, round man with circular glasses and a flustered expression.

"I'm sorry, can I—"

"I'm Charles, Charles Lang? I start work here today. I mean, I'm early, but I'm supposed to start in about forty-five minutes or so."

"Ah, Charles! Welcome, welcome," the man says. His face spreads into a wide grin. "My name's John Doherty. Please, come in. It's a busy day, but please, let me show you around a bit, you know. Everyone's out at a business meeting so introductions will have to come later but you're bound to have other questions, I'm sure."

Before Charles can say another word, John is already bustling back and forth around the lab, naming who works in which office, what research tools are available, etc. Charles is thrilled to see the brand new aquariums lining the walls. He requested them on a whim. He has a feeling that he's going to use them, that they are going to be very important, although he is not sure why or how yet.

"So," John finally says, "what else? What else can I tell you? What else do you want to know? Most of us work in the labs off of this central area, but because you'll be using the aquariums, this will be your primary space."

"What's Peter like?" Charles says. "How approachable is he?"

John's expression darkens. "To be totally honest, I would recommend against that."

"You would recommend against approaching him?"

"Yes, that's what I'd recommend."

"But he's the lab's chief consultant and researcher. Everyone says he's brilliant. And his papers are phenomenal."

John looks back and forth. The lab is empty. "Look, Peter is charming, but he's a total fake. He's cheated his way up to the top. He 'borrows' other scientists' research, if you know what I mean, and then publishes before them. I'm surprised you haven't heard the rumors circling about him. It's why he has such a high turnover rate."

John's confession catches Charles off guard. "I had no idea. Should somebody be told about this? Somebody in a position of authority, who can take legal action—"

"And accomplish what? Peter's the money behind this organization. Sure, we have other investors, but Peter's trust fund could keep Genutech going for another hundred years. Peter may have lied and manipulated to get where he is, but he's also given me the best research position I've ever had. I can't afford to lose it."

"So what—we just pretend that we don't know the truth?"

John shrugs. "That's what I've been doing. It's up to you. If you stay, though, I'd keep the details of your research to yourself. You can give Peter the very broadest of strokes, but no specifics."

Before my conscious mind has even come back into focus, I'm running down the hallway. I heave open the door to the stairwell and rush down the steps, the soles of my shoes barely touching the concrete. I spill into the lobby, nearly tripping over several businessmen sipping their morning coffees.

"Katie? Katie!" I shout as I burst through the glass doors and onto the street. Of course she's gone. A delivery truck grumbles down the road. A flock of pigeons sways back and forth on one of the overhead power lines. I wonder if Katie DeFazio is even her real name. I know that it doesn't really matter if I ever talk to her again, that she's probably told me everything she knows. It's her resemblance to Julie. I close my eyes, imagine Julie bounding down the sidewalk, leaping into my arms. All I want is for Julie to come back, and at this point I would give anything to just see her one more time.

I decide to take the stairs back up to the lab. I want to feel my calf muscles strain as I take one step and then the next. I want to feel the air expand in the soft tissue of my lungs. I want to feel something other than loss. And I want to know. I want to know everything. I'm tired of being deceived. The stairwell smells musky, like rotting fruit long dried and disintegrated. By the second floor, I'm already soaked through with sweat. I take off my coat and tuck it under my left arm. I continue jogging up the stairs. My shirtsleeve catches on one of the splintered banisters and when I pull away, it rips a hole in the fabric.

I reach the fifth floor. As I approach the lab, I hear an argument from inside, words like swords clanging off one another. I recognize the voices as those of Peter and Steve. Peter is in the midst of a rant, his voice bulldozing through Steve's tepid interjections. I try to decipher what they're saying, but it proves impossible without standing right outside the door, and I'm afraid that if I were to do that, I would quickly be discovered. Which is no good given that I'm sure the argument has to do with me.

I don't want to see Peter. I don't know what I would say to him. Now that Katie's left, I feel his betrayal all through me, my body heavy as if the earth's gravitational pull has suddenly become stronger. I keep seeing it in my head, that self-satisfied grin spreading across his face. I just don't get it. Why would he have hired somebody to observe me? What could he want that I wouldn't tell him myself?

I turn the corner down the hallway toward the Human Resources office. Sunlight streams in through windows facing the street. Maybe if I can get some information about Katie, I can find her again. Maybe she does know more than she's told me.

I knock. This time a piece by Chopin wafts from under the door, the two melodies on the piano folding over one another.

"Come in." It's the same middle-aged woman from last time with that glossy updo, typing at a computer. She looks up at me over wire-framed glasses and turns down the music. She seems a bit displeased to see me again.

"May I help you?"

"Yes, Charles Lang. I'm looking for any information you can give me on Katherine DeFazio? Her address, her phone number . . ."

The woman wheels her chair around and opens up the filing cabinet. After a moment of flipping through papers, she shakes her head. "I'm sorry, we don't have a Katherine DeFazio on file here."

"How about Katie DeFazio? She was a research assistant?"

The woman shakes her head again. "No DeFazios."

"Um, well how about John Doherty?"

The woman frowns and thumbs through the files. "Hmm, it seems that the only John Doherty who worked here was terminated in the fall of 2007."

"Terminated?"

"Fired."

"There's no other—"

"That's all I have," the woman says somewhat sternly.

I put a hand down on the desk. "I'm sorry, I'm not trying to bother you, but—"

"What did you say your name was?"

"Charles. Charles Lang."

The woman reaches into a cabinet and heaves out a large cardboard box. "I was just cleaning out the office and found this. Lucky you came in today, otherwise I probably would have dumped it in the garbage. Do you want it?"

I take the box and brush off the dust. Underneath is a piece of masking tape labeled "Charles L."

"Yes. Thank you."

The woman turns back to her computer screen, dismissing me. I step into the hallway and open the box. Inside there's a mug, several books, a small DNA model made of rubber and plastic. They must have cleaned out my room after I left. I continue digging, deep into the crevices at the bottom of the box. Underneath I discover two tiny plastic bags. One is labeled "DNA Sample: Julie," the other "DNA Sample: Jess."

May 19, 2010

Age Thirty-Two

Charles feels his coat pocket again and again, checking that the small plastic bags haven't fallen out. The crinkle is reassuring yet devastating somehow. The stars waver in the night sky, as if they're not sure whether they want to be one thing or another. The beige building looks average, unexceptional under the streetlights. The windows are dark. The shades are drawn. Charles's breath catches in his throat as he recalls the last time he was at the lab, the destruction, the humiliation. It's been four months since he's worked at Genutech and nine months since they disappeared. Nine impossible months. Nine months of comatose days and sleepless nights, brief moments of lucidity followed by horrific nightmares. Nine months of nothingness. It feels strange to him to be wearing clothes, shoes, a scarf, a coat, disguised as a normal person again. It feels strange to breathe in air that's outside, that doesn't have the stale, recycled quality of being indoors.

Before attempting to enter the building, Charles takes the bags out of his pocket one more time. This obsessive checking has become one of many nervous tics. He holds the bags in gloved hands. It's not cold enough for gloves outside, but Charles is paranoid that the oil from his palms will somehow seep through the bags and spoil the samples. The samples are valuable, more valuable than he would have imagined.

Charles was foolish. He washed their dirty clothes. He wiped down the countertops. He tried to remove the remnants of their humanness from the house, only to realize later that these remnants were the very thing that could lead to having Julie and Jess back. He knows that these samples of DNA may already be damaged, that there are risks involved in attempting to replicate these cells. That the results may be undesirable, to put it lightly. But he also knows that he has to try. Any chance is worth the potential repercussions. In Julie's bag, he has the scrapings from a travel razor used long ago. In Jess's bag, a single fingernail clipping from the bottom of her garbage bin.

Charles holds his security badge up to the front door. He has a feeling that it still works, that they wouldn't have thought to limit his entry to the entire building. For a moment, as he raises his hand to swipe the card, he pictures red lights flashing, alarms going off, alerting everybody to his presence. Instead, the tiny light blinks green, and he pulls open the glass door with no issue whatsoever. He knows better than to imagine he can get into the lab. He knows Peter and he knows that he doesn't trust anybody, especially people who have previously destroyed tens of thousands of dollars' worth of equipment. But there may be another option.

Before Peter founded Genutech, there was a larger pharmaceutical company that had labs on the fourth and fifth floors of the building. When that company outgrew the space, they leased the labs on the fifth floor to Peter. Genutech was very small at the time, however, and Peter didn't want to commit to leasing the fourth floor as well. He knew, though, that the lab equipment and the extra space might eventually come in handy. So he worked out a deal with the pharmaceutical company. For a relatively reasonable monthly fee, the pharmaceutical company would keep some of the lab equipment on the fourth floor in place and retrofit the rest of the rooms as offices. The pharmaceutical company could then rent those offices and avoid the issue of having to move or sell the extra lab equipment. Conversely, Peter had the security of knowing that he had a quick, easy option for expansion should Genutech become a larger company. That was the plan, at least.

After several years, however, the lab equipment on the fourth floor became outdated enough that Peter refused to continue paying the monthly fee. The equipment wasn't broken or inoperable, but Peter always insisted upon having the most cutting-edge technology. The pharmaceutical company had enough money at this point that they decided to abandon the situation altogether. Nobody else wanted to deal with the extensive remodeling that would have had to take place if the equipment were removed, so in several of the back offices, the equipment simply stayed. Thus, Charles's plan—even if he can't get into the labs on the fifth floor, there's a good chance that some of the equipment on the fourth floor will be accessible. It may not be the best equipment, but certainly an improvement over nothing.

Charles takes the elevator up to the fourth floor. He reaches into one of his other coat pockets and pulls out a headlamp. He straps it on, flips the switch. A thin stream of light speckles off the wall. Better than the overhead lights. The last thing Charles needs is for somebody to get suspicious because they see the lights on in the middle of the night. Charles is methodical, starting at the very back of the hallway and turning the knobs to each of the offices. The first several offices are locked, not surprisingly, but finally one of the knobs at the end of the hallway turns with a long, satisfying click. Charles creeps into the office to discover that it's empty. Most likely nobody is leasing it right now. There's a small door in the back wall, only about five and a half feet tall. Charles climbs through the door. It's more than he could have hoped for.

Although the lab equipment is in need of a good cleaning, the room is fully retrofitted with several computers, advanced microscopes, a variety of slide sizes, a wall with various chemical samples, etc. He takes the plastic bags out of his pocket. If Charles can't find his wife and daughter, then perhaps he can recreate them. With the discoveries he has made and with the knowledge he now possesses—there's a possibility that he can create versions of Julie and Jess so real, so impeccable in body and mind that nobody would ever be able to tell the difference.

"Hello? Charles, is that you?" says a voice from behind.

Charles freezes. His knees feel like they may give out. Slowly he circles around to face Peter. Peter flips on the overhead lights. Both Charles and Peter turn away from the brightness. Peter has large dark circles under his eyes.

"I, I . . ."

"It's okay, Charles," Peter says.

"I didn't think anybody would be here." Charles clutches the plastic bags.

"Well, it just so happens that this room is right underneath my office. You can hear everything. The floors are very permeable." Peter pauses, then sighs. "I've been sleeping here the past several nights. On the couch. I had an argument with my wife. It seems that my scientific expertise contributes nothing to my success in interpersonal relationships."

"I'm sorry," Charles stutters. He's finding that he's having difficulty with words.

"No matter," Peter says. "Look, you're a good scientist, Charles. A great one. And I don't want to be the one to stand in your way. If you want to come back to the lab, if you think you can—"

"No, I don't think that would be such a good idea." The thought of going back to the lab sends a shiver down Charles's spine. He can't be around people anymore. Not after what happened.

"Well, you're welcome to use the equipment in here whenever you'd like. And if you need anything, please don't hesitate to let me know and I'll have it brought to this room."

"Thanks. That's very generous of you."

"I'm going to try to get some sleep now. If you need me, you can dial up my office. There's a phone in the corner over there. Just make sure to turn off the lights when you're done."

MY BODY DOESN'T FEEL LIKE MY OWN. I FEEL LONG LEGS moving down the hallway. A lead fist reaching up to the door. A brain expanding, swelling. I feel all of these things and yet I don't. I feel as if I'm watching somebody else as I bang against the frosted glass. When Peter opens the door, no words are exchanged. He lets me into the room in silence. Several drops of blood drip down onto the carpet.

"Charles, your nose is bleeding."

I reach up and feel the warm wetness against my fingers. Peter hands me a paper towel. I allow his arm to hover and then wilt in midair. He shrugs, crumples up the towel into his palm, then sits down at his desk.

"You should settle down, Charles," Peter finally says.

"Tell me the truth and I'll leave you alone."

"Look, you don't need to cause a scene. I'm on your side. There's no reason to be angry."

"You had somebody spying on me! What am I to you, some sort of case study?" I slam my hand against one of the counters. A glass beaker rattles and rolls off, cracking on the floor.

"Please, be gentle with the equipment." Peter is grinning, an almost imperceptible grin buried beneath fake concern. The next part feels as if it's happening in slow motion. I step down on the beaker, smashing it in half, taking the largest shard in my hand. Orange sunlight filters in through the window, viscous and bright, the sunshine sticking to my arms and legs. The glass sparkles in the sunlight like slivers of ice. A loose sheet of printer paper flutters against the air conditioning vent. My feet are moving in long, open steps, like an astronaut treading over the moon's terrain. Peter scrambles back against the wall. I don't feel anything. Nothing at all.

"Charles, you don't understand. Let me explain," Peter says.

"How do I know you won't just lie to me?" I pin Peter against the wall with my left hand. "How do I know you didn't have something to do with Julie and Jess?"

"Charles," Peter gurgles. "I would never do something like that."

"Then why were you observing me? Why did you tell me Katie was a therapist? Why are there cameras in my lab and house?"

"Because you're a scientific miracle," he says. "Because you're alive."

"What is that supposed to mean?"

Peter squirms. "Please, if you could just let go of me."

"What is that supposed to mean?" I repeat, louder this time.

Peter's gaze is deep and penetrating. "It means you were an experiment. It means you're not real." I tighten my grip. He spits in my face. The slow motion sets in again as I raise my right hand. Only this time, just as I'm about to plunge the shard of glass into Peter's shoulder, something cold and heavy hits me in the back of the head. The world goes blank.

September 5, 2011

Age Thirty-Three

The air is still as a stone. There's no traffic passing outside. Everybody has gone home. Charles checks that the legs on the tripod are secure, then adjusts the lens of the video camera. He's rented stage lights for the occasion, small ones that are still very hot. The bulbs sizzle in their chambers. Charles can feel the sizzling on his skin. The collar of his shirt constricts around his neck, a snake squeezing the life out of its prey. He turns away from the lights and takes a deep breath, another, another, calming himself down. Charles is both more nervous and more excited than he has ever been before. He's about to make history, while at the same time transforming his own life so thoroughly that it can never be the same again.

Charles stands back from the camera. He turns the screen so he can see the image of himself that the camera is taking in. He's surprised by his image. He looks so put together, even as he's falling apart inside. He's still a young man at thirty-three, still boyish in certain ways, still handsome. He wears spectacles pushed too close to his eyes, a blue checkered shirt, khaki slacks, brown wingtips, a starched white lab coat over everything. His eyes are so bright that they look like planets, glimmering with the light from the stars. His blond hair is buzzed short and his face is clean-shaven.

Charles checks behind him to make sure everything is in order.

A body lies on an examining table, covered by a thin sheet. Next to the table there's an IV stand and an EKG. The EKG blips every moment or two. The body's heartbeat is steady, calm. About two dozen wires run from underneath the sheet to a large computer, going in one side and coming out the other. At the end of each of the wires is an electrode. Images flash across the computer screen at more than twenty per second. Charles takes one more deep breath, closing his eyes. He thinks about Julie and Jess. He sees a picture of them against the backs of his eyelids. They are out in the woods, on one of Julie's favorite hikes. Jess is no more than three years old, and she's just discovered the pleasure of worms. Julie is splattered with mud from having helped Jess dig in the wet earth. Jess has so many earthworms in her hand that it's impossible to count. When Charles opens his eyes, he pushes the picture away. It's still completely unreal to him, the knowledge that after tonight, if everything goes according to plan, he will never think about Julie and Jess again. He will finally be free from the memories, the loss. A small part of him questions if he wants to be free, but he pushes that thought out of his mind too.

Charles checks the battery level of the camera, adjusts the lights. And then, without taking another moment to reconsider, he presses the record button. He watches the red blinking light for several seconds. He clears his throat, tilts the camera back a smidge. Once the words start, Charles is surprised by how easily they flow out.

"Hello, my name is Charles Lang and I am a molecular geneticist at Genutech. The date is September 5, 2011, and I am thirty-three years old. I'm recording the final steps of this project because should everything go as planned, I may not be in a position to record the results afterward.

"For the past several years, I have been engaged in a series of experiments involving cellular transdifferentiation, molecular cloning, and three-dimensional printing. Two of my most significant findings are as follows. First of all, through close examination of the jellyfish species Turritopsis dohrnii, *the 'Eternal Jellyfish,' I have deciphered the precise mechanism through which their mature adult cells are able to transdifferentiate to become other types of mature adult cells, a process that cuts out the tedious necessity of stem cells. I have since been able to induce this process to occur in the adult cells of a variety of animal organisms. Using a sample of adult cells from any animal organism, we can use the process of transdifferentiation to grow new cells programmed to be heart cells, lung cells, liver cells, or any other type of tissue.*

"Secondly, I have discovered that the part of the DNA molecule previously thought of as 'junk' actually contains coding for memory. These sequences aren't necessarily useful all on their own. However, through my research, I've determined that the memory of an individual can be transferred to another being using a computer that can translate the language of these DNA sequences into audiovisual memories. These audiovisual memories are then stored on the computer and can be transferred to another individual through the use of a hippocampal prosthesis. The hippocampus is part of the brain's limbic system and plays an important role in the formation of new memories about experienced events, called the episodic or autobiographical memory. Thus, implanting a hippocampal prosthesis, or artificial hippocampus, would allow for the transfer of episodic memories from one person to another."

Charles opens his palm to show a model of a hippocampal prosthesis to the camera. It essentially looks the same as a computer chip. Charles then reaches behind him and pulls the sheet off of the body on the table. It is a man, who appears to be in a deep, peaceful sleep. The man is an exact clone of Charles. The contours of his naked chest rise and fall with each breath. He looks as real as any other human being.

"I introduce you to the 'other' Charles Lang, who I will hereafter refer to as CL," Charles says, gesturing to the body on the table. Charles pulls up a shirtsleeve to reveal a thick layer of scar tissue across his own right arm. "The cell samples necessary to develop healthy, viable organs were extensive, and even using three-dimensional printing technology, it took almost a year to create CL. However, CL is now well equipped for life. He is constructed totally of transdifferentiated cells, with the only exception being the hippocampal prosthesis implanted in his brain. For all intents and purposes, CL is a human being no less real than you or me."

Charles pours himself a glass of water from a nearby pitcher. He takes several gulps. There's a heaviness in his tone as he continues. "This isn't a flawless process, and unfortunately before CL, there were numerous cloning attempts that proved far less successful and had to be terminated. I hope the same is not true of CL, but I acknowledge this as a possibility. Science is imperfect, and it is only through this imperfection that we are able to improve and grow. I hope that those who later stand to judge me will weigh the ethical risks of this experiment against its likely contribution to the betterment of humanity."

Charles stops again, takes another sip of water. His hand is shaking. "The most ambitious of the previous experiments took place between May 19, 2010 and January 17, 2011, and involved the use of cell samples from Julie Lang and Jessica Lang, who I will refer to as J-1 and J-2 for the purposes of this discussion. Due to the use of faulty samples, including partially damaged cells and DNA molecules, J-1 and J-2 emerged from the incubation chamber with severe observable physical and mental deformities and were only able to survive for several hours.

"Initially, I believed that the faulty samples were also the cause of the subjects' extremely limited capacities in encoding, storing, and retrieving memories. However, upon examination of the subjects during the autopsies, I was surprised to find that both subjects had fully matured brains that should have been capable of much more advanced memory processes. This was when I came to realize that DNA molecules could not in and of themselves be used to transfer memories but rather needed to be translated by a computer and downloaded onto a hippocampal prosthetic. Moreover, while I haven't yet deciphered the biological explanation for this phenomenon, I have determined that the DNA molecules of a deceased person cannot be translated and thus cannot be transferred to another individual. At this time and with our current methods, we cannot resurrect the memories of the dead."

Charles points to the computer behind him. "Therefore, as mentioned, memory content can be uploaded and transferred from one living organism to another, so memories can be transferred from me to CL. Using the program that I've developed, I can even be selective in which memories I transfer to CL. And finally, by using the same computer program to deliver small, targeted electric shocks, I can select and delete specific memories from my own hippocampus."

Charles sits down in the desk chair. He fastens a vast web of electrodes to his scalp. There is already a crown of electrodes attached to CL's shaved head.

"When I flip this switch," Charles says, pointing to something similar to a light switch at the edge of the computer monitor, "an intense wave of electric voltage will flow between me, CL, and the computer. CL will inherit copies of all of my memories, while I will delete from my own mind all memories dealing with my family and my scientific career. This transfer will cause CL to emerge from his artificially induced coma. And upon this emergence, he will be me. He will become Charles Lang. And I will be somebody else.

"You may ask why I have programmed it so that I will lose what others may consider to be my most valuable memories. The truth is that I don't want to be Charles Lang anymore. I want to start a new life with new memories. With my memories, CL will be able to take over my duties as one of the world's most influential scientists. He will have the celebrity, the money, and the honor. And I will be able to lead a quiet, happy life, away from all of the memories that have haunted me, especially my memories of Julie and Jess."

Charles fits the last electrode into place. He breathes in and smiles. "So thank you to everyone who has made this possible, and may today become one of the most significant in scientific history."

Charles flips the switch. At first there is nothing but a low hum. The hum grows higher in pitch. And then, suddenly, everything is distorted. Charles and CL both begin convulsing. The lights crackle and pop as the bulbs blow up, spraying glass across the room, briefly illuminating a face in the door's small window. Charles's body jumps and jerks against the chair, a frothy mix of spit and vomit bubbling from his mouth. CL's head seeps blood as he falls from the table. The video camera crashes to the ground. The computer overheats, sparking and sending smoke into the air. Someone bursts in through the door and it's Peter, who has been watching through the window. He flips off the switch. Everything goes dark for several moments, as if the entire world has shut off.

And then I am there, for the first time. I am in a memory for the first time. My eyesight feels blurry, my limbs weak, my body freezing. I'm lying naked on the concrete floor, and every part of me hurts. Peter runs over to me and detaches the wires from my head. As he holds me up, I see Charles, Charles who just moments before was young and handsome. His hair is singed around the electrodes, fluids staining the collar of his blue checkered shirt. He lies unconscious in the debris, and he appears to have instantaneously aged fifty years, his skin dry and wrinkled, his features sinking into themselves.

I feel myself slipping in and out of consciousness. I look up at Peter, his face chopped up and segmented like a Cubist painting. Before he can say anything, I drift away into a black, expansive sea of nothingness. And it is this nothingness, this emptiness, that is the beginning of my life.

PART IV

July 9, 2006

Age Twenty-Eight

A hiking trail winds up through the hills behind the house, surrounded by vines growing thick as pythons, shrubs scattered dry against the ground, trees crawling on top of one another, grasping at something unattainable. Charles and Julie stand at the foot of the trail, poised, about to race. The sign reads Birch Lake Pass.

Charles's face is scruffy, sandy stubble like pebbles against his chin. He wears a plain white T-shirt and khaki pants. Julie has her hair pulled back into a bun. She wears a patchwork jumper that makes her look like a child again. Jess is strapped to her back in a carrier, giggling in the sunshine, a hat protecting her cheeks and neck from the summer's heat.

Julie plants her feet in the dirt, turns to Charles and flashes him a small, mischievous grin. Then, like a jackal, she begins sprinting through the forest, Charles soon following behind. They plunge through the trees, the forest coming alive around them, a breathing creature, the colors vibrant and shifting, the trees yawning in the afternoon light. Charles reaches out, again and again, never quite able to catch up to Julie and Jess, Jess howling with laughter at the bumpy ride. Finally Julie arrives at a clearing at the top of a cliff overlooking the lake. The feeling of eternity stretches around them as small waves lap against the shore where they so often sat together as children, as gulls swoop through the sky, as the plants around them unfurl and stretch. Charles catches up and he and Julie whirl around together, scooping Jess up in their arms so that she can see the entire world. They collapse on the felted grass around them, heaving in deep open breaths.

Charles holds Julie's hand in his, feels the warmth of her flesh, feels the wedding ring against his fingers, and he remembers the day they first ran up this hill, remembers stooping down on one knee and sliding his mother's ring on Julie's finger. He can think of no place he would rather be, of no family he would rather have in his life than this.

❧

"CHARLES?"

Time cracks apart. I feel myself fragment, the pieces cracking into fragments themselves. A dust storm of memory whorls through my mind, shattered images raining down on a wasteland. The images land like tattoos on my skin, four birthday candles smoking as Jess blows them out, a worried furrow across Julie's face as she tries for the last stroke on an almost-finished painting.

"Charles?"

The voice lingers in the air as I look around, Steve's voice, but I'm no longer in the lab, I'm running home along a deserted sidewalk, streetlamps glowing orange through a cold, impenetrable fog. My mind reengages with the environment around me. My knees buckle and I fall, landing on the dewy grass of somebody's well-manicured front lawn. I begin to cry, throaty sobs from deep in my chest, sobs that cause my whole body to shake, my cheeks streaked with salty tears. None of this has been mine. This isn't my life. These aren't my memories. I'm a nonentity. All along I suspected, knew that these weren't my memories, that I was watching them from a distance as an observer, an outsider. The truth is that I'm only the echo, a servant indentured to the memories, the tragedy, the loss suffered by the first Charles Lang. I've never even met Julie or Jess, not really. I don't have a history of my own. I have nothing from before I woke up in the laboratory, before I woke up on the couch in the living room, nothing that couldn't be somebody else's. All I've done is borrow someone else's life.

I hate Charles for his selfishness, for his recklessness. But most of all I hate that every moment I've experienced with Julie, Charles has gotten to experience in real life. I hate that he got to feel her skin against his face, that at night, he said to her, "I love you," and Julie said it back across the bed. I hate the first Charles Lang—I hate him with every part of me, because even if it's only through his memories, even if I've never met her before, I've fallen in love with Julie.

I've fallen in love with the sweep of Julie's hair and the one dimple in her right cheek. I've fallen in love with her creativity and talent and the depth of her instinct. I've fallen in love with who she is and who she has the potential to become. I've fallen in love with her image, and yet I've fallen in love with *her* too. Whoever Julie is beyond the memories, I know that I love her to my fullest capacity. I hate the first Charles Lang for thrusting on me a predetermined existence that has no hope for anything but sadness and mourning. But I understand him too. I hate Charles and understand him at the same time. The memories he experienced, the pain they invoked—how can I blame someone for wanting to run away from that?

The back of my head throbs, and when I touch my sticky hair, I find that the blood is still wet. I'm reminded of the pain I felt from where the electrodes burned my scalp. I thought that pain would never dissipate. Suddenly I realize I'm breathing hard. The memory of what just happened returns to me in chopped images, mental photographs pieced together. I remember holding Peter against the wall. Waking up sprawled on the floor. Steve standing over me with a round-bottomed flask, flecked with blood. Peter locking himself in his office. Steve telling me to stay put, that he was going to get some bandages from the other room. And then I was running, running as fast as I could, down the stairs, out the door, my vision slipping and crackling like a film at twelve frames per second, the night distorted, the stars swimming around me.

I'm on my knees on someone's lawn. I take a breath and look up. There she is, standing in the middle of the street, watching me. The moonlight reflects off of Jess's hair, her cheeks rosy pink like a doll's. She wears saddle shoes and pom-pom socks, a pink princess dress and a little white sweater. She smiles at me, waves when my eyes catch hers, and I slowly rise, mesmerized, taking one step forward, another, my breath steaming in the night. Jess takes a step backward, another, stumbling.

"Charles?" the little girl says, her pigtails bobbing against her head. Jess's face melts away, replaced by Ava's ridge of freckles and fiery red hair. She looks up at me, at my hopeful arms, still outstretched. Smoke curls out from a nearby chimney. I shiver with the cold of the night air.

"Charles? Charles, what happened to you?" I hear a baby crying, howling from far away. The world sways. And as I look at Ava's delicate figure before me, I wish I could have held Jess just once, could have felt her small, warm body tucked against my shoulder.

August 23, 2004

Age Twenty-Six

The curtains flutter against the windows. Charles jolts awake with a sick feeling in his stomach. The blackness of night is just beginning to warm into a deep purple-blue, and Charles immediately reaches across the bed to find the sheets cold and abandoned. He hears a loud moan from the bathroom. His bare feet thump against the hardwood as he runs down the hallway. Julie squats on the bath mat, her knees up to her chest, her back to the door. There's a pool of wetness around her, seeping through her nightgown, and in the darkness, Charles can't tell if it's water or blood. Charles crouches down next to Julie and she clutches him against her, leaning and sobbing into his shoulder. He rubs a soft hand against her back while taking her elbow, helping Julie to her feet. He knows what's happening and they cannot stay here. They must get to a hospital, before it's too late.

"It's not time yet, Charles, it's too early," Julie wails as Charles leads her to the car, a trail of fluid dragging behind her. Her face is swollen, her eyes chapped and puffy. Charles has never seen her so distraught before. He can't feel anything. He cannot allow himself to feel anything right now.

"It's okay," Charles says as he lays Julie down in the backseat. "It's all going to be okay."

Julie looks up at him. "What if I lose her?" she says, her question somehow accusatory. "What then?" Charles remains silent. He doesn't know how to respond. This isn't supposed to be happening. She's at least five weeks early. Charles turns on the car radio.

"Turn it louder," Julie says. Charles turns the volume loud enough to discourage any thoughts, any fears, turns it so loud that the words of the song become static in their ears. The streets are empty in the early morning, with only the shriek and lights of a passing ambulance rippling through the stillness.

When they reach the hospital, everything flashes by in a blur. The emergency room, the nurses, the doctors. Julie gets whisked away to the delivery room just as her mother arrives. Mrs. Hollingberry wafts into the hospital like some sort of fairy-tale creature, a loose, flowing dress sifting around her body. The doctors direct her and Charles to the waiting room. Julie has insisted on being alone. Not even Charles will be allowed in until after the birth.

Mrs. Hollingberry and Charles share a cherry Danish and an instant coffee from the vending machine, watching the sunrise through the narrow windows. They're the only ones in the waiting room except a lone janitor swooping his mop across the floor. Mrs. Hollingberry's gaze drifts toward the ceiling, searching for something. Charles wonders if Mrs. Hollingberry realizes why Julie wants to be alone. That Julie doesn't want anybody else to see if the baby is born dead.

After several hours of reading Newsweek *and* Time, *absorbed in speculations about the November elections, Charles turns to Mrs. Hollingberry and taps her on the shoulder. For hours she has been staring out the window, her eyes hardly blinking. It's as if something of her is no longer there. She doesn't seem to be herself.*

"Do you think it's a bad omen? That the baby's this early?" Charles says. Mrs. Hollingberry's eyes are almost violet, sparkling in the morning light. Charles folds his hands together, twisting in his plastic chair. Even though he asked, he doesn't want to hear the answer. Normally Charles isn't one to believe in these things, omens, fate, and prophecies. At the same time, however, the sick feeling in his stomach persists, and there's something noxious about the air around him. His thoughts are polluted as he imagines Julie screaming in pain, blood pouring over the bed, a gray infant body resting between her legs. He sees no future without them.

Mrs. Hollingberry doesn't respond.

"Mr. Lang?" It's one of the doctors, a young man with thick blond hair and a wide smile.

"Yes?"

"Congratulations. Your wife has just given birth to a healthy baby girl," he says, reaching out to shake Charles's hand. "Because she was born prematurely, your daughter will have to be kept overnight in the neonatal ICU for observation, but so far, everything looks great."

Charles exhales. He's in a haze as he follows the doctor and Mrs. Hollingberry down the hall. Charles takes Julie in his arms, planning never to let go. Mrs. Hollingberry watches from a distance, murmuring something under her breath to herself.

"I don't know what I would've done if . . ." Charles feels Julie against his cheek. Her skin is so pale, dark circles under her eyes, but she is more beautiful than she has ever been.

"Shhh. It doesn't matter now," Julie says, nuzzling Charles's shoulder. A nurse walks into the room with the baby in her arms, freshly cleaned and wrapped in a white blanket, her eyes sealed shut.

"Would you like to hold her?" the nurse asks. Before he knows what he's doing, Charles is holding his daughter, a baby so small she's hardly bigger than a honeydew melon. He holds her against his heart, feels her faint breaths. She feels like nothing, and a part of Charles is afraid that if he blinks, she'll disappear.

"Jessica."

"What?"

"I think we should name her Jessica, after my mother," Julie says. "What do you think? We could call her Jess for short." Charles turns around to discover that Mrs. Hollingberry has vanished from the room.

"Yes, of course." Charles holds Jess in one hand and squeezes Julie's shoulder with the other.

Later that day, when Jess has been taken to the ICU for observation, Charles sits in the recovery room, watching Julie sleep. He feels himself close to drifting off when he notices a book of baby names on the counter next to his chair. He takes the book, flips it open. The name "Jessica" appears on the first page:

> *"Jessica, based on the original Hebrew name Yiskāh (יִסְכָּה), means 'foresight,' or being able to see the potential in the future."*

And for a moment, Charles wishes he could just know. He would give up excitement, give up surprise, he would give it all up if he could just be sure that everything was going to be okay.

~

I COME TO ON THE COUCH IN IRIS'S LIVING ROOM, A wool blanket tucked around my chest. Iris stands at the stove, still in her baby blue nurses' scrubs. Steam swirls up around her as she stirs a pot of chicken soup. Ava sits perched on my thigh, her feet disappearing under her skirt like a mushroom. Her face is inches away from mine, her lips slightly parted, carrying an intent expression. I can tell she's been sitting there, waiting, watching for me to open my eyes.

"I thought you were dead. You just fell down, like—" Ava makes a splatting motion with her hand. I notice my right arm, the sleeve rolled up, the scrape on my elbow red and brittled from the asphalt. "It was really scary."

I take Ava's hand in mine. Her small fingers wrap around my thumb.

"Ava, sweetie, can you go start getting ready for bed? PJ's, teeth, you know the drill. It's already way past your bedtime and you have school tomorrow," Iris calls from the kitchen.

"Can Charles sleep at our house tonight? And can we have blueberry pancakes in the morning?"

"We'll see. Now go brush your teeth."

Ava swings her legs off the couch and lands on the floor with a slight thump. Before she ducks into her bedroom, she plants a small kiss on my stubbled cheek.

Iris sets the soup down in front of me with a wedge of

French bread. "It's hot but you should be able to eat it without burning your tongue." The aroma of dill and rosemary is intoxicating and I have to resist licking the bowl clean when I'm done. Meanwhile, Iris settles herself down on the couch next to me. She slides off her white orthopedic shoes. Her face is the lightest of pastel pinks. "Are you all right, Charles? Because if you're not—"

"You don't have to worry about me, Iris. I'm sure I was just dehydrated."

"Oh yeah? And what about the gash on the back of your head?"

I touch the spot, just above my neck. The wound has been cleaned, covered with a swatch of gauze.

"Do you know how many bits of glass I picked out of that? What happened?"

"A fight. But everything's okay. Really."

"Is it? You're falling apart, Charles, and last time that happened, you disappeared."

I pause. "I miss them, that's all. Julie and Jess. I keep thinking about them. All the time."

Iris sets a hand on my arm, her gaze drinking me in. "Look, I understand, Charles. Believe me, I do. It's not like I stopped loving Rory once he died. But you're still a young man. You still have a full life ahead of you, if you just let yourself stay in the present."

I sink back, full and sleepy. "Did I ever tell you the story of how I proposed to Julie? It was our first time hiking up Birch Lake Pass, out by Mount Christie. The yellow and orange wild flowers were just starting to bloom and when we got to the top, the day was so clear that we could see all the way out across the lake until it descended into the horizon. I knelt down and my knee sank into the silty mud and I slid my mother's ring onto her finger. I felt so sure, Iris. How am I ever going to feel that sure again?"

Iris's expression falls. "Did you say Birch Lake Pass?"

"I remember the sign. The one in blue letters with the hand-painted sun in the background, right?"

"And you're sure that's where you proposed to Julie?"

"Yes. What's this about?"

Ava calls out from the other room. "Mom, I'm ready for you to tuck me in!"

"One moment!"

Iris turns her attention back to me. "Maybe it's nothing."

"But?"

"But it's just that last year, when I did that hike with you and Ava, I could have sworn you said you'd never been there before."

"Mom?" Ava stands in the doorway, wiping at her eyes. She wears matching pajama tops and bottoms, light purple speckled with a universe of silver stars.

Iris takes my empty soup bowl and sets it on the countertop in the kitchen, then scoops Ava up into her arms. Before whisking Ava down the hallway, Iris turns to me and says, "It's been a long day, Charles. I very well could be remembering wrong. I could've sworn, though . . ."

I SPEND HOURS THAT NIGHT STARING UP AT THE CEILING, at the grooves undulating across the paint. Shadows from the trees outside waver like witches gathering in the nighttime. A black cat clock ticks above the sink, water dripping from the faucet. Iris sleeps in the other room, small sighs just approaching snores. I try not to make any noise as I tie up my shoes, folding the wool blanket into a neat corner on the couch. I leave a note on a Post-it on the fridge, the chicken scratch handwriting barely legible, and let myself out the back door without a sound. The night air sits crisp against my face, like the first bite of an apple. I like the feeling of being alone, of knowing that everybody else is asleep.

When I let myself into the house, I immediately sense something's wrong. All the lights are off and I hear the loud rush of water from the bathroom, too loud. My shoes crunch against something hard. I look down and staring back up at me is the fractured face of a marionette, its blue eyes and blond hair a near replica of myself. The body has been split in two, the wood splintered like monsters' teeth. Marionette parts are strewn across the floor, limbs and bodies and strings, clothes torn, tossed aside, the remnants of a massacre, the last of the marionettes finally wiped out. My heart beats in my throat. I avoid the rest of the marionettes and approach the bathroom.

Charles sits on the toilet lid, scrubbing remnants of blood out of the bowl of the sink. He hasn't yet noticed the splatters on the floor. His left wrist is wrapped in gauze. A razor leans up against the toothbrush holder, the blade already sparkling clean. He looks up at me, his eyes like pools of water, a murky image of myself distorted by ripples. I look at him, crouched over the sink, nothing but fear, and I realize he's less human than me at this point. There's something so diminutive about him, so defeated and hollow. Earlier this evening, lying awake and seething with anger at mistaking Ava for Jess, I tried to plan something to say to this Charles. I wanted to be cruel, to punish him. But seeing him again, I realize there's nothing left. He's tissue paper floating in the wind.

I take the washcloth from Charles's hand and turn off the faucet, guiding him from the bathroom to the living room couch. I tuck the blanket around him as one might swaddle an infant. He seems barely aware of what's going on. When he attempts to speak, nothing comes out. Einstein appears from the darkness, circling and plopping himself down in Charles's lap. A film crackles on the old black-and-white TV, Cary Grant and Deborah Kerr embracing at the end of *An Affair to Remember*. They wipe the tears off of one another's faces as they kiss, Grant's chiseled jaw against Kerr's smooth and creamy skin.

"Don't worry, darling," she says. "If you can paint, I can walk. Anything can happen, don't you think?"

I wake up the next morning on the living room rug, tangled among a shamble of pillows and blankets as Charles sleeps on the couch, his breath coming out in little tufts of air. Einstein cuddles into his chest, cooing in time with each breath. A sheet gathers in a tangle at Charles's feet. I pull it back over his shoulders. He twitches slightly with a dream. I wonder what he's dreaming about. I wonder what it would be like if I could see into his mind, if he even realizes who I am.

I pack a bag for the day—a brown bag lunch of peanut

butter and jelly, a thermos of coffee, my wallet, a foldable umbrella. Black storm clouds roil in the wind, like charcoal smeared against the sky. Before I leave, I gather anything that Charles may use to hurt himself. I take the knives from the kitchen, the razors and pills from the bathroom. I pass the marionettes, the loose bits of string scattered across the floor. Their faces express everything and nothing at the same time.

The air outside is brisk and cool. Leaves swirl around my feet. I concentrate on my steps, on the way my shoelaces curve around one another as if they're holding hands. Finally I reach my destination, the stairs of a public library near Ava's elementary school. It's an ornate brick building in the colonial style, two white Ionic columns as sentinels beside the front door. I made a mental note of the library's location the first time I passed by, imagining that it may be of use at some point. For someone at the forefront of modern technological research, it has seemed unusually hard for me to connect with the outside world, but the library is an answer to this, an emporium of books, microfiche, and interconnected networks.

I pass by the novels and collections of Ray Bradbury and Isaac Asimov, of Kurt Vonnegut and Philip K. Dick, and my heart longs for these familiar words. Images flash across my mind, men burning books in blazes of fire, robots hurtling through the skies, World War II veterans whipping through time, electronic sheep bleating from the rooftops. I want to sink into one of the brown leather armchairs with a dozen books in my lap and never move again, never acknowledge the outside world. I want to escape into the words of others, words that would allow me to pretend to be human and happy and loved. Instead, I continue to the back room where Jurassic-age computers are hooked up to cables coiling around the tables' legs.

I've decided that I will no longer be complacent. I will find out what happened to Julie and Jess. I reason to myself that there's nothing to lose, since if I never know what happened to them, I'll only assume the worst. I imagine Julie here with me, sitting at the computer across from me, flipping her dark hair back as she grins, chewing the end of her pencil. I imagine Jess flying up and down the children's aisle, her leaps and bounds like a dance, taking every book on ballet that she can get her hands on and flopping into her mother's lap. I shake my head. A cursor on the computer pulses, waiting for me to make my next move, the bright Google logo uncomfortably cheery as I type in, "How do you find out if someone is dead?"

I glance over my shoulder, at an old lady humming to herself, at a group of young moms reading to their toddlers, hoping nobody has seen what I typed. I wonder what I would think if I came upon someone who wrote what I just did, if I would judge that person, if I would find the question unsettling. But for all I know, there's no mystery to what happened to Julie and Jess. Perhaps the mystery only exists in the world of Charles Lang's mind, the only mind to which I have access.

I click on a link to the Social Security Death Index. It takes me to a page where I'm asked to fill out information for a search. The questions are objective and uninvolved, and I can't help wishing there were more to be asked, more than their first and last name, their date and location of birth. What was her greatest wish? What was his deepest secret? What did she dream about at night? What was he most afraid of? My hands shake as I type the information into the form. I realize how little I know about Julie, about a woman whom I love yet who is barely more than a name to me. I don't know when she was born, nor where, though I can guess. All I know is Julie, Julie, Julie.

I breathe out a deep sigh as I press the enter key. The first list has over one thousand people. Julie M. Lang. Julie Lynn Lang. Julie A. Lang. Women who have died in Ogle, Illinois, in Miami, Florida, in the Bronx, in Missouri, in Ohio, women who died fifty years ago and young girls who died a week before. I shift the mouse, click "Refine Search," limit it to women born between 1973 and 1983. I try again. The closest to come up is a "Julie H." who died in California in 1996, ten years before my Julie disappeared. I click on the link, wanting to know this other Julie, wanting to know where she was born, how long she lived, her cause of death, if she was happy, if she was fulfilled, if she believed there was meaning in life. But of course, the website cannot tell me any of these things. All it can tell me is that there once was a Julie H. who died in California in 1996.

I type in Jess's name now, willing the computer to go faster. The results pop up onto the screen. The only Jess Lang died in Boulder, Colorado in 1986. I release a breath long held, the air claustrophobic in my lungs, forgotten within me. I must have been loud because the old man sitting at the table across from me puts his finger up to his mouth in a shushing gesture. But if only he could know the relief that I feel, that at least there is a possibility, however small it may be.

I refresh the browser and navigate to the missing persons section of the police department website. Blurry, pixelated people stare back at me from photographs, pleading with me, wishing to be found. The first is a man named Robert Vincent Butler, an old man in a plaid shirt leaning back in a rocking chair. I click on the photograph and here the details are abundant, more than I expected. Male, age sixty-four, of Caucasian descent, six feet, 170 pounds, gray hair, brown eyes, reported missing on March 21, 1998. The circumstances: "Mr. Butler was despondent over his health. On the day he was last seen he failed to keep a medical appointment. Mr. Butler may be a patient of a medical facility or be in the care of a boarding facility."

I click on another photograph, a black-and-white photograph of a young girl with a bright, mischievous grin on her face, two front teeth missing, a tabby cat nestled in her arms. Karen Lane Jacobs, female, age eleven, of African American descent, black hair, green eyes, four feet eleven inches and only 55 pounds. She was reported missing on November 18, 1961. The circumstances: "The missing person was last seen on November 18, 1961, at approximately 3:00 p.m., leaving the Ridgewood Elementary School grounds. The missing person was en route home where she was never seen again." I close my eyes and try to think about what she would look like now, how her face would have transformed with age, sleek and seamless in her late teenage years, fuller and more mature in her twenties and thirties, a few wrinkles creeping in around her forties and fifties before people began to think of her as wise in her early sixties. This woman, this child, would be over sixty years old if she were still alive. In the time she has been missing, she would have gone through adolescence and adulthood, motherhood and her middle years. Or maybe she didn't see any of this part of her life. Maybe the last day she saw was November 18, 1961, and she has been left to linger like a ghost on this list.

I imagine what it would be like if they were on this list, Julie and Jess gazing back at me, Julie crouched on the living room floor, Jess curled in her arms, sticky paint all over their fingers. Their information would be listed just like everybody else's, first Julie and then Jess. Julie Lang, female, age thirty, of Caucasian descent, five feet seven inches, 130 pounds, brown hair, hazel eyes, reported missing August 23, 2009. Jess Lang, female, age five, of Caucasian descent, three feet four inches, 39 pounds, brown hair, hazel eyes, reported missing August 23, 2009. The circumstances: "The missing persons were last seen at their home residence on the evening of August 22, 2009, at approximately 8:30 p.m. The next morning they were no longer at the house. They have not been seen since."

But then I blink and they're not there. I check two, three times. Julie and Jess are not on the list. Instead, in front of me, I see a round, blotchy male face, familiar somehow. His eyes are like beads of dark matter, his mouth pulled back into a toothless smile. I recognize the name: Bruce Kerman. Male, age forty-eight, of Caucasian descent, five feet ten inches, 210 pounds, brown hair, brown eyes, reported missing on September 25, 1986. The circumstances: "Mr. Kerman was last seen at Ridgewood Elementary School on the morning of September

25, where he shot and killed eight-year-old Gordon Howe before fleeing the crime scene. Mr. Kerman has a history of mental illness including antisocial personality disorder. If he is spotted, please call 911 immediately."

October 7, 2008

Age Thirty

A teacher stands at the front of the classroom, her students gathered in a hush on the rug. The children squirm like caterpillars, restless, perhaps wondering why they weren't allowed to go to lunch. One child bolts for the door but discovers it's locked. Only Jess sits still among them, her hazel eyes sparkling green in the sunlight until the teacher pulls the shades shut. Jess is by far the smallest of the children. She's a year younger than everybody else, only four years old. Normally the school wouldn't have allowed a child so young in kindergarten, but she was so precocious, so mature, there was nothing else for them to do. Charles sits in the back of the room, watches the teacher straighten her blouse. He was supposed to speak to the class for career day, tell them why they should be excited about science.

The teacher, Mrs. Henry, clears her throat. She struggles to maintain her composure, wipes her mouth, smudging her lipstick. "Now class, you may be wondering why you're not allowed to go to lunch and why some of your parents have started to gather outside.

You may wonder why there was an ambulance earlier today and why the flag is only raised halfway up the pole. And you may have noticed that Benjie's not here."

The students look back and forth, suddenly aware that Benjie is missing. When the teacher continues, there are tears running down the little crevices in her cheeks.

"At recess today, Benjie fell off the monkey bars and had a very bad accident. The ambulance took him to the hospital but it was a very bad fall. And I'm afraid that Benjie is in heaven now."

Jess raises her hand, gazing down and picking at the carpet's fibers at the same time.

"Jess?"

"How come Benjie didn't say good-bye?" she asks.

"Unfortunately, sometimes there isn't time to say good-bye."

As the teacher continues to speak, Charles starts forward and scoops Jess up in his arms. He holds her tiny body against his chest. Charles wishes this moment would never end, feeling Jess's heartbeat against his, protecting her from everything bad, even as he senses that she has already become tainted. She's still so young, and yet she is already doomed.

I UNPLUG THE COMPUTER, THE IMAGE OF BRUCE KERMAN sizzling off the screen. The teacher's words echo through my ears: *Sometimes there isn't time to say good-bye*. But maybe there can be. Maybe there still is, and the only way to know is to find out what happened the night Julie and Jess disappeared. They could still be alive, they could be out there, even if they're not on the missing persons list. But of course, the logic of it is hard to justify. What causes people to disappear and never come back? If this were a Hollywood movie, the answer would be easy. They were abducted, held hostage, brainwashed and such. But the more likely possibility is that if Julie and Jess are still alive somehow, they probably don't want to come back. They wanted to disappear. I don't like to think about this option, because if they were escaping from Charles, they were escaping from me. But I push all of this away, shove down the gnawing feeling in my stomach. I'm not Charles. I'm not the same man, and I can still hope for something. At least that hasn't been taken away from me yet.

I head to the school next. Ridgewood Elementary, two blocks away. They must have some sort of school records on file. There must be somebody who knows something. The wind snaps around me as I exit the library, dark storm clouds brooding above, still pregnant with rain. I pull my coat in closer to my neck, wishing the sun would peek out. I feel I could use it, today of all days. A thick fog filters through the school yard with the trademark chill of the Pacific Northwest. The children don't seem to mind, though, and they continue with their games of handball and Chinese jump rope.

"Hey Mr. Lang!" a voice calls out, and a small boy runs up to the fence. He has a nest of blond hair flopped down on his head, and his sweatpants have holes in the knees.

"Hi," I say, giving an awkward wave.

"It's me, Leo. I'm friends with Ava. We have playdates sometimes," he says, slightly out of breath.

"Of course, I remember you, Leo," I say, although I don't at all.

"Did you move back to town?" Leo asks. "Ava and I never got to do the volcano experiment you said you'd set up in your backyard."

"We'll have to get to that." I give a half smile, not managing a full one. "Say Leo, what grade are you and Ava in?"

"I'm in fourth grade. Ava's in third."

"I know it's a long way back to remember, but can you recall if there was a girl named Jess in kindergarten with you?"

Leo squinches up his face to think. "No, I don't think so."

"Jess Lang?"

"No, cause we would've sat next to each other since I'm Leo Lucas."

"You're sure?"

A red handball bounces toward Leo. "I've gotta go. I wanna play before recess is over."

I nod to Leo as he runs back across the asphalt yard, lined with tan bungalows and ficus trees. There's a grassy lawn out in front, an American flag blustering in the wind, and a sign on the double doors leading into the school, reading: "Parents and/or Guardians of Currently Enrolled Students, please type in the access code on the dial pad to the right. Other visitors, please schedule an appointment with our receptionist in the main office. You must have an appointment to come onto school grounds. Thank you!"

I peer in through a small glass window in one of the doors, tapping against the glass. An older African American woman in a navy blue blazer looks up from her paperwork in the main office, then glances back down again. The fluorescent lights glint off of the laminated ID card fastened to her pocket. I press the buzzer by the side of the door. Nothing. I knock on the window again, harder this time. Nothing. I begin pounding against the door with my fist. Finally the woman rises from her desk chair. Even from outside I can hear her heels clack against the linoleum floors as she walks toward me. Instead of letting me in, though, she leans over and opens the mail slot at the bottom of the door.

"Can I help you, sir?" she says, a crinkle in her voice.

I crouch down, look into the set of gray eyes that stares back at me. "My daughter used to attend this school. Jess Lang. I need to access her school records."

"I'm sorry, sir—"

"Charles. Charles Lang."

"Mr. Lang, you need to make an appointment to come onto school grounds."

"I swear—it'll only take a moment."

"Policy is policy."

"What if you got the records? I could stay out here. You wouldn't have to give them to me. You could just tell me what they say. Please."

"And when did your daughter attend Ridgewood Elementary?"

"She was in kindergarten for the 2008–2009 school year. Jess Lang. She was technically too young, but they let her in because she was precocious."

"Right. She didn't continue on to first grade?"

"She went missing after that."

The woman sighs. "Look, Mr. Lang, I wish I could help you. But we're not going to have her records anymore. We only hold onto student records for two years after they stop attending Ridgewood."

My knees wobble. I put a hand down to balance myself. "And then what happens to them?"

"You'll have to contact the district offices for any further information. I'm sorry, I have to get back to my paperwork."

"What about you?" I plead. "Did you know her? Jess Lang? Does the name sound familiar?"

"I'm afraid I can't help you, Mr. Lang. I've only been working here for about six months." And with that, the woman lets the mail slot clatter shut behind her as she returns to the main office.

Discouraged, I abandon the double doors, pacing by the classrooms as students file in from recess, sweaty and disheveled. I imagine Jess sitting in one of the stuffy classrooms, completing worksheets in addition and subtraction. I imagine her gathering with the other students on the rug for story time, playing board games on rainy days and carrying too many picture books at once in her backpack. She had friends. She would have been the type of girl who didn't care what her peers thought and thus was cool and popular in their eyes. And she would have had secrets, secrets that I would never know.

I round the corner. Tucked away behind a chain-link fence, there's a garden filled with rosebushes beginning to bloom. It's a memorial garden. A placard in the ground reads For Gordon Howe, bordered by a bare plot of dirt and a blank placard, as if the garden has been waiting for its next addition. Bouquets of flowers rest on the ground below Gordy's placard. An invisible hand squeezes my chest.

I turn away from the garden, looking instead at the mural that they are painting on one side of the school. It's a cloud of fairies upon a stage, dancing and twirling around one another. A gawky boy in green tights stands center stage, his brown hair up in a cowlick. It's a still scene from the school's production of *Peter Pan*. I search for Jess among the fairies, hoping for just one glimpse, and for a moment, I spot her in her ballet slippers and turquoise leotard, swirling around the young boy in green tights. But a moment later, her image shifts before me. It's not Jess in the mural but Ava, her hair bright red against the turquoise, a spray of freckles across her face.

November 2, 2011

Age Thirty-Three

A dream. Charles crouches down in the depths of the night, his face the alabaster white of bone. He is in his living room, and yet wisps of artificial branches and forest leaves crawl around him. A chorus of children's voices breaks from the distance. A stage light snaps on behind Charles, buzzing louder and louder as it gets brighter and brighter. Charles sits on the hardwood floor and holds his knees against his chest. The chorus grows closer, their voices distorted, crashing over one another like cacophonous waves, their throats raw and rasping.

"Now repeat after me—I won't grow up!"

"We won't grow up!"

"I don't want to go to school!"

"We don't want to go to school!"

"Just learn to be a parrot!"

"Just learn to be a parrot!"

"And recite a silly rule!"

"And recite a silly rule!"

The chorus surrounds Charles, their warm, sweaty bodies crowding in around him, and Charles realizes that they are the Lost Boys from Peter Pan, *barefoot and dressed in rags, mud smudged across their cheeks, a malevolent gleam in their eyes. They stomp up and down in time with the music, rattling the hardwood floor beneath them, as their ringleader comes out, Peter Pan. His felt hat tips down over his face as he carries a bundle of a blanket in his arms. Peter Pan looks up as he spits out the next line of the song. Charles discovers that Peter Pan is not a boy at all, but—*

"Julie? Is that you?"

Julie is no longer a woman but a girl, small and diminished, a paltry version of her former self. She refuses to acknowledge Charles, screaming out for all to hear: "If growing up means it would be beneath my dignity to climb a tree, I'll never grow up, never grow up, never grow up, not me!"

"Not I!"

"Not me!"

"Not me!"

Julie looks Charles directly in the eye, and with a snarl, she lets free the blanket, revealing a mess of shattered glass and blood held within. The Lost Boys vanish. Julie leans in, whispering into Charles's ear: "I'll never grow up, never grow up, never grow up . . ."

Raindrops slide down the back of my neck, like fingers. I pull up the collar of my coat around me. I don't move. I can't bring myself to move. Finally, when the water has begun to cling to my eyelashes and soak through the cotton of my shirt, I tear my gaze away from the mural and continue toward the lab. The wetness seeps through my shoes as thunder and lightning crack the sky apart. I walk the several blocks down to the lab, the storm growing, fat drops of water slapping against my back, as a part of me wishes it would just wash me away, down the street and out to the ocean. I could float away, alone with my thoughts. I could disappear into the horizon.

I arrive at the familiar building, the beige paint turned brown in the rain. I stand outside the sliding glass doors as I did my first day, watching the doors glide open and shut as they wait for me to cross the threshold. I need to talk to Steve, to find out if there's anything else he may have forgotten to tell me. I imagine the people of the town around me, tucked away into offices and apartments, schools and houses, their lives a vast, interconnected web of social interactions and relationships. My world, by comparison, is so small and dense that sometimes it feels like I can't breathe.

The elevator is out of order so I slog up the stairs with zombie footsteps, the concrete reverberating throughout my bones. Panic flares up inside of me as I stand in front of the doors to the lab. I realize for the first time the gravity of what I did to Peter. He could have me arrested, charged with aggravated assault. I could go to prison. But somehow I don't care. My existence is singular—to find out what happened to Julie and Jess. I force air in and out of my lungs, pushing the panic away. I have to talk to Steve. I don't care about anything else right now.

I try my key card. The light blinks red. I try again. Red. Once more. The light blinks red but the door cracks opens this time. Steve peers out, his green eyes orbiting around the hallway until they land on me.

"Charles—"

"Can I come in?"

"You shouldn't be here."

"Is Peter—"

"Home for the day. The bruises on his neck are still pretty swollen. But you know how he is—he could pop in at any time. And if he sees you—"

"Please, Steve, all I'm asking for is a few minutes."

Steve gives one last cursory look around the hallway, then motions for me to follow him in. "Just a few minutes, though. It's for your own good."

I'm surprised by how normal it feels to be inside the lab again, how comforting I find the sterility, the antiseptic smell, the rooms whitewashed in fluorescent lights. Steve leads me into his office, shuts the door behind him. His desk is cluttered with manila folders, manuals, and books. I sneak a glance at one of the titles—*A History of the Microbiology of HIV and AIDS.* He has several diplomas on his walls from the University of London, as well as a number of framed photographs. The majority of the photographs are of Steve and Richard, a tall, handsome man of Indian descent, dressed in a tweed coat with a smile bursting at the seams.

Steve takes his glasses and wipes them on the edge of his shirt. When he puts them back on again, his pupils seem magnified as they stare through me.

"How's your head?"

"Still painful."

"Let me take a look," he says.

"It's fine."

"I'm not asking."

I lean my head over the desk, wincing as Steve pulls up the back of my cap, the bandage around my head soaked with dried blood.

"Don't move," he says, getting up and retrieving a first aid kit. He slowly cuts the bandage away, treating the wound with hydrogen peroxide and fresh gauze.

"It could've gotten infected, you know. You have to be very careful about these things," Steve says. He looks at me with the kind of serious regard that doctors reserve for their patients. "Why are you here, Charles? Believe me, I'm happy to see you, and you know how much I care about you, but you shouldn't come back to the lab anymore. Not after what happened with Peter."

"You know I'm not really Charles."

Steve pauses for a moment. "I know," he finally says.

"And it wasn't my fault. With Peter."

"Look, I'm not here to make judgments. I don't need to take sides. I just want to help, if I can." Steve finishes up with the gauze, packing up the first aid kit and stowing it in the cabinet.

"Steve, I'm here because I want to know what happened to Julie and Jess. So if there's anything you haven't told me, anything at all . . ."

Steve rinses off his hands. "There's nothing left for me to tell. Charles never really spoke about their disappearance to anybody at the lab. The old Charles, I mean. We didn't even know anything had happened until a few months after the fact, and we had no idea about the severity of how it affected him until he had the breakdown at the office. He was very private, even with me."

"Were there any news articles about it? Any press coverage?"

"No, nothing, which is odd, of course. Charles must have done everything he could to keep the incident out of the media, maybe even paid them off?"

"But you started working here before they disappeared, right?"

"Yeah, I started working here six months earlier, in February 2009."

"And you didn't see them at all during those six months? For dinner or . . ."

Steve sits down in his desk chair, setting his chin against his left palm. "No. I didn't see them. Charles didn't say it specifically, but it seems that Julie felt very betrayed when I left for Europe, perhaps deservedly so, and was still pretty angry with me even after all those years."

"Six months, though, that's a long time. There was no attempt at reconciliation? Or Jess, you didn't meet her?"

Steve sighs. "I haven't told anybody this before, because I'm not sure at all that it's true, but I considered the possibility that maybe Charles was purposefully keeping Julie and Jess away from me. That it was Charles's decision, not Julie's."

"But why would he have done that?"

"I'm going to be blunt," Steve says. "That kind of controlling behavior, of trying to isolate Julie and Jess—these are patterns often seen in situations of domestic abuse."

"Which would also bring up the possibility that Julie and Jess ran away, that they disappeared on purpose."

"Right." Steve takes off his glasses again, massaging the spot on his nose between his eyes. "But I really don't think that was the case. I grew up with him. We were best friends. And I just can't imagine Charles would do that."

"Do you think there's any chance that Julie and Jess are alive?"

"I suppose there's always a chance until you know otherwise." Steve plays with the wedding ring on his left hand, a silver band engraved with his and Richard's initials.

"Steve?"

"Yes, Charles?"

"What happened after I—well, before the other Charles and I returned to the house?"

"Peter and I took care of you. You both nearly died. We nursed you back to health until you were well enough to be sent home. Peter was devastated by what happened to the other Charles. By his decision. By the aftermath. Peter didn't have many friends and he cared a lot about Charles."

I feel sick in the pit of my stomach as I think of what I must be to Peter, an artificial approximation, someone only approaching personhood. I stand to leave. "Thanks for the help. I'll try not to stop by here anymore."

Steve puts a hand on my shoulder. "Charles, there's something I need to tell you."

"What?"

Steve folds his hands together, his fingers mashing against his knuckles. "When we came into the lab yesterday, the jellyfish were dead."

"All of them?"

"All of the ones in the experimental condition. We're still investigating the cause of death. It's possible that there was some sort of contamination that led to infection, and the fact that they underwent cellular transdifferentiation was just happenstance—"

"But?"

"But we've also detected signs that their skin was beginning to atrophy and that neural communication was starting to deplete."

"So what does that mean?"

Steve pauses. He glances up at me with his seawater eyes. "Look, it may mean nothing at all. There is that chance. But it's more likely that there were flaws in the experiment, that the process has not yet been perfected. And since you're the product of a derivative process—"

"How long?"

"There's no way to know."

"If you had to guess, Steve."

"I would guess that it would be about a year before you begin to notice any symptoms, about two to four years before total system shutdown. It could be far more time than that, but it could be far less."

I stare down at my fingers, still long and angular, just as they were before. "What's it like?"

"What's what like?"

"Going home to Richard at night? Falling asleep in each other's arms? Knowing that you're loved?"

Steve becomes aware of the ring again. He touches it briefly, then slides his hands into his pockets. "We broke up, about two months ago. It just wasn't working out . . . we didn't talk anymore. And I guess as long as I keep wearing the ring, I can imagine that things can go back to the way they used to be. Richard, I don't know, but it's the idea of him, the idea of who he used to be—that's who I'm still in love with."

February 16, 2005

Age Twenty-Seven

Charles stands in the middle of an empty room, his socked feet sinking in the carpet, his gaze locked on the right-hand corner of the wall. He can hear everything from downstairs—Jess's sleepy infant whimpers, Julie reciting an old nursery rhyme, the white noise machine, Julie's footsteps as she climbs the stairs. He knows he should be doing something to help, washing bottles, taking out the trash, but he can't bring himself to move. Instead, his eyes remain fixed on the two names carved into the plaster: "Jonathan and Grace Forever, 1975." There's a small heart beneath the names, pastel pink, perhaps once brighter in the past.

Charles tries to imagine what his parents were like at that age, people with first names, giggling lovers who believed they would be together forever, who didn't realize how soon, how young they would be together in death. He wonders what they were like before they were parents, free from the expectations and responsibilities of raising a child. He has always imagined them as reserved, judgmental, curmudgeonly for their age. But over the years he has discovered photographs, tucked into drawers, under mattresses, in hardback novels, photographs suggesting that they once lived carefree and uninhibited, that they once had dreams, believed anything was possible. He feels their presence in the room, whisking, dancing around the carpet, threatening one another with still-wet paintbrushes, brand-new bedroom furniture waiting for them in the hallway.

Charles remembers going to the park as a child, his mother pushing him on the swings, his father lifting him up onto the slide. He remembers their excitement at his high school graduation, arriving early so that they could get seats in the very front of the audience, his father leaning down on one knee, taking photograph after photograph. He remembers their apprehension upon moving him into his freshmen dorm, his mother wiping down the surfaces to make sure they were clean, his father fixing a squeaky spring in the bed, apprehension that came from fear, the fear of losing their son to the world.

Charles sits down on the carpet, rocking back on his heels, his eyes still fixated on the names on the wall. He wonders what his life would be like if his parents were still alive, if they could have been at his wedding, if they could have been at their granddaughter's birth. Charles thinks of the dreams he has, the ones in which his parents are alive once more, the ones in which they are always dying, always haunted by images of their former selves.

Julie pads into the room, puts her arms around Charles's shoulders. "Why do you think babies cry so much?" she asks, kissing him on the cheek. She smells like baby powder and diaper cream.

"Because they can feel all the sadness in the world," Charles says. Julie turns Charles so that he's facing her. She sees the crinkles at the corners of his eyes.

"You've been up here for a long time." Julie squeezes Charles's hand.

"Yeah, I know. I don't think I can come down."

"Do you want me to help you?" Julie asks, and Charles lets her guide him out of the room, down the stairs, into the living room. She opens a window, letting in the cool night air. The crickets call out to one another. A gentle wind swishes through the trees.

"We can't do it," Charles finally says, lying prostrate on the couch. He lifts his legs so that the blood will flow back into his head. "I don't think we should put Jess's bedroom up there. Or ours for that matter."

"It wouldn't have to be anytime soon," Julie says, stroking Charles's forehead. "She's still so young. We have years ahead of us."

Charles sits up. "Look, I know it may not seem rational, but it doesn't feel right. The second story. There's death everywhere, I can feel it around me. We have enough space. We don't need the second floor. The second floor was theirs."

"So what do we do? We don't have the money for any big renovations," Julie says. Charles stands, eyeing the staircase, flat up against the wall.

"What if we just boarded up the staircase? All it would take would be some lumber, some plaster, some paint. I could do it myself."

Julie hesitates. "I suppose that could work."

"I wouldn't ask this of you if I didn't think it was important. Jess doesn't need to start her life already steeped in memories of loss and death."

"I know, Charles. Believe me, I know," Julie says. "But we can't protect her from everything, you know. At some point we're just going to have to let go."

I FEEL A STRANGE LABYRINTHINE DIZZINESS AS I LEAVE the lab, winding my way down the stairs and out onto the street again, the maze of the town crushing down on me as I weave in and around passing pedestrians. I'm not so concerned about the possibility of a premature death, and I realize I never really expected to grow old. In spite of the intensity of my emotions, my physical vulnerabilities, the fact remains that I'm not human in the typical sense of the word. The myths of the life cycle, a treasured childhood, a tortured adolescence, settling down in middle age to have children and a family, retiring from one's career, the gradual deterioration that comes with old age—none of these describe my life, my entrance into the world. My memories are like images reflected back on broken glass, brilliant and meaningful but still not the actual experiences themselves. If anything, my conversation with Steve, the prospect of my own mortality—these only magnify the need to find out what happened to Julie and Jess, to be able to find peace within myself.

My next stop is the tavern that Julie's uncle owns. I slosh through the tattered leaves and twigs along the sidewalks, saturated with rain. Every moment of uncertainty brings more questions. Where was the last place Julie and Jess were seen? Who was the last person to see them? Could they have been abducted from the house? Have there been any false leads? Did something precipitate their disappearance? I think back on my conversation with Steve, and I again confront the fact that Charles's memories may not be entirely reliable. There are times when his memories of Julie and Jess somehow feel too good to be true, and I don't know how to see such love without expecting disappointment or something worse.

I find myself in familiar territory, the folksy charm of the little enclave around the tavern. It seems untarnished by the present until I begin to notice the For Rent signs plastered in several shop windows, the waste bins overflowing with banana peels and crumpled newspapers. A family of European tourists pauses in the middle of the narrow street, posing for a photograph. I realize that what seemed like some sort of mystical fairy-tale escape had in fact been designed that way, meant to entice people into buying handcrafted tchotchkes at inflated prices. It seemed so enchanting in the nighttime, transcending the mundanity and regrets of real life.

I walk down the steps to the tavern, the dark wood creaking with each footstep. The air is dense around me, smelling sour, yeasty, different from how I remember it. A group of old men sit together at a table in the corner, eating enormous plates of bratwursts and spaetzle, speaking in loud, broken German. The paintings are different too, strange, idyllic landscapes of the German countryside before World War I. A bartender stands behind the counter, a slim man with an antelope face wearing lederhosen and a felt hat. I approach him and he turns, giving me a friendly nod.

"Can I help you, sir?" the bartender asks. "We have an extensive list of beer and a really excellent currywurst."

"Thanks, I'm actually looking for somebody, the owner of the bar? His name might be Mr. Hollingberry? I'm not 100 percent positive on that."

"Do you mean Eduard?" the bartender says. He crosses his arms. "May I ask what this is regarding?"

"Tell him it's Charles, Julie's husband," I say, and the bartender pivots, disappearing into the back. I expect an older gentleman to emerge, someone tall with bright white hair suggesting its once blondness. Instead, a young man appears, his reddish curls gelled into a peak, his teeth crooked as he puts out a hand.

"Charles, it's nice to meet you. Why don't you follow me into the back and we can chat?" Eduard suggests, and he leads me through a hallway and into an office, cluttered with receipts and file cabinets, a bookshelf filled with leather-bound German classics, a shelf with antique beer bottles. I sit across from Eduard's desk in a dilapidated plastic folding chair, hoping it won't collapse.

"Sorry for the mess, it's just been quite a transition the last month or so with my father's illness. I suppose you were expecting him?" Eduard says. His voice is slightly accented, somewhere between German and British.

"I suppose. I don't know, I don't know what I was expecting," I say. "This may seem like a funny question, but do we know each other? Sometimes I have a hard time with those sorts of things."

"No, I don't think so. I grew up in Germany and I've only been living in Washington for about one month. Now you'll pardon me for asking my own funny question, but should I know who Julie is? You mentioned that you were her husband?"

I'm taken off guard. "Julie Hollingberry? She was Rolf's daughter? We used to come here all the time. I thought you would have known her."

"Ah." Eduard pulls open a small refrigerator behind him and brings out two bottles of beer, handing one to me. We tap the bottles together before cracking off the lids. The beer's mild, tasting slightly of lavender, cool and refreshing against my throat. Eduard lights a cigarette and takes a long drag.

"I'm sorry, but I don't know Julie. I don't even know much about Rolf, for that matter, other than that he moved to America and passed away many years ago."

"So your father—"

"Axel. Rolf's older brother and apparently Julie's uncle. He was the one who used to own and manage the bar before I took over."

"And you grew up in Germany?"

"Yes. Soon after I was born, my parents split up and I stayed in Germany with my mother while my father moved to America to be closer to Rolf. This was when Rolf was very ill, and then my father never came back. Of course, now that my father is sick and dying himself, all he wants is to return to Germany. In times of tragedy, we want what our memories tell us to want," Eduard says, taking another drag from his cigarette. "But who am I to judge? You taste the lavender in your beer? The favorite flower of my childhood."

"I'm sorry about your father." I don't know what else to say. There's a moment of awkward silence as I take another sip from my beer. I try to hide my frustration, my guilt that all I'm really thinking about is myself. Every possible lead becomes a dead end, every obstacle increasingly insurmountable.

"Unfortunately, my father's not doing very well and isn't in much of a state for visitors these days, but maybe I can help you in some way?" Eduard tries.

"I'm looking for information about Julie and my daughter, Jess. They've been missing for over two years. I know it must seem foolish, to try to find them now, but if they could still be out there—well, is it possible that you have the contact information for anyone else who may have known Axel or Rolf back in the day? "

"One moment." Eduard shovels through the desk, tossing aside crumpled budget sheets and order forms. He curses to himself through puffs of his cigarette until at last he unearths a well-worn Rolodex. He shakes out the dust and sings to himself as he flips through it, looping, breathy phrases of German. Finally he pulls out one of the cards, the phone number almost illegible through a dark coffee stain. He hands it over to me.

"Jessica, erm, yes, Jessica H.? Does the name ring a bell? I could have sworn my father once said she was his sister-in-law."

My heart flutters. "Yes! I mean, yes, she was, Jessica Hollingberry, Rolf's wife. Julie's mother."

Eduard smiles. "Great! Well, you will have to give her a call."

"Do you know anything about where she might live these days? About what happened?"

Eduard stands, lights another cigarette and paces back and forth, his face obscured by a veil of smoke. "Ah!" he exclaims after a moment. "It all comes together. I have been in the States for many years, since I was eighteen, but I used to live in New York City. One time, when I was here visiting my father, I remember helping him pack up a woman's house. She was moving somewhere further south, Arizona or Nevada or . . . I didn't realize who she was at the time, but it must have been Mrs. Hollingberry, after Julie disappeared."

February 28, 2010

Age Thirty-Two

Charles hears the moving trucks before he sees them, feels their vibration as they rumble past the house and stop at the corner. It's been days since he's really gotten out of bed, almost a month since he's worked at the lab, a month since his breakdown. Charles's pajamas are sticky and sour against his skin. His bedroom is littered with discarded food wrappers, the little bits and pieces he's forced himself to eat. The only thing that keeps him going is Einstein, who rests his squashed, orange tabby head in Charles's lap.

The curtains are pulled tight, protecting Charles against the sun's invading rays, and when he stands, stiff and sore, and pushes the curtains aside, he's surprised that the world has continued to go on around him. A neighbor takes his husky on a walk. A young boy sits bundled up in his mother's arms. And down the street, in front of Julie's childhood home, two moving trucks idle outside, their tail pipes pouring steam and diesel fumes into the early morning air. The moving men slouch on the porch, taking notes on a clipboard as Mrs. Hollingberry stands in the doorway, sipping a large thermos of hot tea, wearing something in between a long coat and a robe. Charles watches as the men enter the house and bring out wide card-board boxes, stowing them in the back of one of the trucks. They take furniture as well, couches and floor lamps, canvases wrapped in thick brown butcher paper to protect the paintings inside. She's moving. She's actually moving. Charles wonders if Mrs. Hollingberry planned to say anything to him or if she was just going to leave, let him discover the change once a new family moved in.

Charles shakes his head and grabs his coat from the chair. He knows he looks terrible, that his hair is in tangled thickets and that his beard is growing in shabby, stubbly patches. He knows his breath must smell awful and that he should change into something besides his wrinkled pajamas covered in cat hair. He knows that he's a mess and that with every step he takes, he'll feel the sharp, biting pain of losing Julie and Jess. He knows these things and yet he cannot let Mrs. Hollingberry just disappear. They've hardly spoken a word to one another the past several months. Perhaps they haven't spoken at all.

When Julie and Jess first went missing, Charles and Mrs. Hollingberry consoled one another, kept each other company through the long nights, were open and honest about their emotions. But slowly they grew apart, each believing the other was somehow to blame. Every day Charles became more convinced that Mrs.

Hollingberry had known what was going to happen, that she had seen into the future yet failed to prevent it. Mrs. Hollingberry, of course, vehemently denied this power of foresight, not in all circumstances but certainly in this one, and she harbored the belief that Charles was responsible, accusing him of pushing Julie and Jess away. And then there was the matter of the funeral, a funeral that Charles refused to have. Mrs. Hollingberry couldn't forgive him for this, for failing to lay their souls to rest. For Charles, a funeral would mean he had to stop looking. And until he found them, he would never stop.

As Charles trudges down the street in the chilly morning air, wishing he had worn something more than slippers, he realizes he has nothing to say to Julie's mother. He's still angry, and he imagines she is too. But when Charles sees her up close, standing in the doorway of a house that will soon no longer be hers, he finds that she's just as diminished as he is. She's even thinner, frailer than she was before, to the point where she seems capable of breaking at any moment. Her coat is gray and drab, and the makeup she wears is protective, trying but failing to conceal how much she's aged over the past six months. When she sees Charles, she nods to him, neither smiling nor frowning. They stand next to one another, not saying anything, as they watch the movers take the furniture from the house. Finally, when everything is packed away, Mrs. Hollingberry turns to Charles. She gives his hand a squeeze.

"Good-bye, Charles," she says.

Charles tries to speak, but instead he remains silent, nods his head. There's nothing else he can say at this point.

I CALL MRS. HOLLINGBERRY FROM THE PHONE IN Eduard's office, the plastic curlicue cord twisted through my fingers, the ringing shrill and abrupt, reverberating through my whole body. Eduard has excused himself, ducking into the storeroom to check on the inventory. My breath feels both hot and cold inside my chest. Nobody picks up, just an answering machine. A metallic voice says that the number I'm trying to reach is currently unavailable and to leave a message after the beep. I hear myself stutter as I speak, my tongue a foreign appendage. I manage to croak out that it's Charles. I ask for Mrs. Hollingberry and give her Iris and Ava's number if she'd like to call me back. I know that I should say good-bye to Eduard, thank him for his help, but instead, I sneak up to the tavern and slip through the raucous crowds of German tourists.

I head out into the brisk night air. The rain has dissipated but black snarls of thunderheads still loom overhead. The winds begin to howl, screaming like harpies, the darkness sinking in around me. I have no idea where I am. The town has transformed into forest and underbrush, the mulch squishing under my shoes, the tree limbs weighed down with rain, bending in the wind. I look up at the stars peeking out through the clouds, hoping for help, but I don't know what to do with them, these yellow flecks in the night watching me like eyes. I turn around and blindly select a direction to follow, hoping that it's the right way. I hear the heaving of thunder, a deep, throaty growl, and then the sky breaks open, the rain pouring down in torrents like I've never seen. There's no keeping the water out of my eyes, my nose, my mouth.

I trudge farther into the wilderness. I squint my eyes for a light, a house, a car, any sign of town. But I'm swallowed by the trees, the wasteland. The rain grows so dense around me that I can't see even a few inches forward. I hold out my arms, grabbing in front of me, trying to gain my bearings, and then my foot slides and I catch an unearthed root with my hand. My feet dangle in midair, my body hanging down into a deep ravine, and somehow I'm able to pull myself up, slathered in mud, tears streaming down my face. One more step and I would have fallen to my death.

Shaken, I keep walking as the underbrush thins out and a lake spreads out before me, the water churning, a lone dinghy toppling under the waves. A long, wooden pole leans in the ground, a battered sign reading Birch Lake Pass.

August 22, 2009

Age Thirty-One

Charles wakes up tangled in the covers, his eyesight bleary, the moon a yellow crescent in the night sky. He hears rustling beside him and turns to discover Julie lacing up her tennis shoes, wearing a pair of sweatpants and a hoodie, pulling her hair back into a ponytail. But Julie doesn't look like Julie. She looks like Iris, freckles across her face, her hair auburn, her stance more heavyset. Charles doesn't seem to notice, though. He rubs his eyes and looks at the clock. It's already midnight.

"Julie, sweetie, what are you doing?" he asks, his voice thick and groggy.

"I can't sleep, and neither can Jess. She's been up for hours."

"Have you tried giving her warm milk? Or turning on the radio?"

"We'll be back soon." Julie leans down to tie her other shoelace.

"Come back to bed, Julie. It's too late to be hiking."

"Not a hike, just a little walk around Birch Lake. We'll be careful."

"Please?"

Julie leans in and plants a kiss on Charles's forehead. "Go back to sleep, darling, and I'll come snuggle with you when I get home."

Jess stands in the doorway, waiting for Julie in a pair of light-up Velcro sneakers. Except she doesn't look like Jess. She looks like Ava.

"Just be safe, okay?" Charles is too tired to know what else to say, too tired to even be fully awake, and he rolls over in the bed, closing his eyes, falling into nothingness.

Charles wakes up alone the next day, wakes up to the sound of rain. At first, he thinks that maybe Julie and Jess are up early, that they're out running an errand, out for breakfast. But there's no note. Jess's bed isn't made. The car is in the driveway, and when Charles checks the hamper, Julie's hiking clothes aren't there, nor are her tennis shoes back in the closet. After calling the police, Charles steps into the bathroom, lathers up his face with shaving cream, and as he drags the razor across his cheek, he cuts himself deliberately, just to feel something. But the pain isn't enough. Why didn't he stop them? Why didn't he know? When the police arrive, two burly men with grizzly voices and grizzly beards, Charles finds that he can't speak. His words are like a snake, slithering back down his throat.

I LIFT MYSELF OUT OF THE MUD, RUNNING, CLEARING snarled roots and vast, swampy puddles. Why did Julie and Jess look like Iris and Ava in the memory? I can't even begin to come up with an answer for this. The rain roars around me, beating my face, my back. My wet shoes suck against my feet with each step I take. Nobody else is out. Everybody is home. The asphalt along the road smells like chemicals and earth, the trees twist in the wind, the grass is drowning, silt and debris flood the storm drains. I see Iris and Ava's house in the distance, light pouring out of the windows like warm honey, the shutters chattering against themselves like teeth. I splash across the driveway, the water up to my ankles, and as I climb the stairs up to the porch, the rain turns into hail. A particularly large hailstone dents the hood of a nearby car. Another clatters off the mailbox.

Iris answers the door, her hand over the receiver of the phone, her forehead knit into a furrow. "Charles, are you okay? There's someone—"

I take the phone from Iris, the line crackling and rasping until a faint voice breaks through from the other side.

"Charles? Is that you? Charles?"

"Yes, it's me."

"It's been so long. I never thought I would hear from you again."

Mrs. Hollingberry sounds like a porcelain vase about to shatter apart. I look down at my feet.

"It hasn't been that long, has it?"

"Over fifteen years."

"Fifteen years?"

"Since I moved down to New Mexico . . . are you okay, Charles? You sound . . . well, I'm concerned."

A feeling like seasickness sways through my gut. "You've been living in New Mexico for fifteen years?"

There's a hesitation from the other end. "Yes, Charles, in Santa Fe. I moved there after Julie died. You know that."

It takes all the effort I can muster to speak again. "After Julie died?"

"After Julie died in the car accident. You're sure you're all right, Charles?"

The phone drops from my hand and clatters against the hardwood.

October 22, 1996

Age Eighteen

Charles sits at the small wooden desk in his dorm room, working quietly and methodically on a problem set for genetics. His room is sparse, austere—a thin twin mattress with gray bedding, a dresser filled with folded socks and shirts, a poster of the periodic table of elements above the desk. Charles stands and walks over to the window to try to push it open farther. Although it's late October, the weather is unseasonably warm for

Northern California. Charles wears checkered boxers and a Star Trek T-shirt. A pair of navy pants and a white dress shirt lie draped over the head of the bed. He has the radio tuned to the World Series game, the Yankees versus the Braves, although Charles doesn't really care about the outcome.

He told his parents there was no need to come for the weekend. It was a long drive and there wasn't much to show them. Besides, the campus would be overrun with other parents dawdling around. But Charles's mother insisted on coming anyway, and that was that. Charles certainly couldn't tell her the truth, that he wished they would never visit, that he was tired of his father being sick and of his mother pretending everything was fine. He wishes Julie were coming instead. He hasn't seen her for three months now, and even though they talk all the time, he wants nothing more than to see her face, to look into her eyes, to hold her in his arms. The last time they spoke, she said she had something to tell him. Something she wanted to wait to share until they were together.

Charles gets up for a glass of water and checks the clock over the dresser. He was so absorbed in his problem set that only now is he realizing his parents are over two hours late. Just then, Charles hears a knock on the door.

"One moment!" he calls out, yanking on his pants. The shirt will have to wait.

When Charles opens the door, however, it's not his parents but the dorm's residential advisor, an awkward girl with a blond ponytail and freckled cheeks. She tries to speak but every time she opens her mouth, nothing comes out.

"What's going on?"

"There's a policeman here. He wants to talk to you." As Charles follows the girl down the hall, his mind runs through all of the offenses he committed in the last week or so. He's not a bad person but a mischievous one, and he and his cohorts in the engineering department have spent the past several months one-upping each other with various pranks. Could it be about the swimming pool? Or the sheep brain gone missing?

The police officer takes off his hat and clutches it in his hands when he sees Charles turning the corner. His face is pale, ghastly. And instantly Charles starts to feel sick. He wants nothing more than to run the other way. But instead Charles stands there, entrapped.

The next thing Charles remembers, he is at the scene of the accident. He must have blacked out. He doesn't know how he got there. Sirens cut through the night air, the area cordoned off with yellow tape. He pushes through the firefighters and the paramedics, his hands shaking so hard that he can barely walk. All he wants to do is look away but he can't. He sees large claws of jagged metal twisted in on themselves. A rubber wheel engulfed in flames. The accordion hood smashed in, the front bumper contorted into a mangled frown. Shattered glass from the windshield, shards like teeth crunching under his feet against the asphalt. His parents' bodies have already been removed from the car, zipped into black body bags, stowed in the ambulance. But Charles sees Julie's reflection in the glass from the windshield, bloody and fragmented, her lips blue without oxygen, splinters of bone and gray matter stuck to the seat cushions, a single eye still open, the pupil dilated. Julie wasn't supposed to be in that car. She wasn't supposed to come, to surprise him. Charles turns and before anybody can say anything, he sprints away from the accident, into the trees by the side of the road, as fast as he can, as far as he can, not wanting to believe, not wanting to think.

It's only later that Charles finds out what Julie wanted to tell him in person: she was pregnant. A girl, four months. It wasn't supposed to happen this way. It wasn't. It wasn't . . .

❧

THE NEXT THING I REMEMBER IS RUNNING UP THE driveway, a large swathe of purple wisteria against my back. I rattle the key in the front door but the lock is sealed shut. I pound my fist, yelling to be let in. Finally, I throw myself against the door with a leap. The wood splinters, my sleeve ripping as I hurtle into the entryway. The room is silent, dark in a thick and airless sort of way. Something is different. I realize that all of the marionettes are gone.

"Charles? Charles!" I call through the house, turning on the lights. I don't know why I didn't realize the truth sooner. No missing persons report. No news articles. No school records. No photographs. Julie didn't go missing three years ago. Julie died in 1996, at the age of eighteen, the fall of Charles's freshman year of college. Every memory of Julie after that was a fabrication, a delusion. And Jess? Jess was never even born. Maybe, deep down, I knew the truth. Maybe I knew but didn't want to believe it.

I wind my way back to the entryway. In the wisps of moonlight that break into the house, I discover a set of paw prints, caked in white plaster, leading to a bookshelf by the front door before vanishing. I steady myself, squaring my feet and lowering my center of gravity, ready to heave the shelf aside. But when I push against the side panel, the shelves immediately slide aside with no resistance. I take a book from the shelf, examine its empty husk. It's fake, they're all fake, hollow on the inside. I push the bookcase aside and of course, it's there, it's been there all along, a hole in the wall, about three feet by three feet, the drywall crumbling along the edges. I crawl inside and begin climbing the stairs to the second story, dusty, wooden stairs that creak with each step. My hair stands on end. I wonder if I'm hallucinating the smell of smoke in the air. But with each step I take, the smell grows more acrid and pungent. And it's warmer than it should be.

"Charles?" I call out again. The upstairs is small, more like a studio apartment, with a bedroom, bathroom, and closet. The carpet in the bedroom is matted and stained, with imprints of where the bedposts used to sit. Cobwebs drape in the corners and the only furniture in the room is a large wicker trunk, lid open, spilling over with old patterned housedresses. Smoke pours out of the bathroom, clinging to the ceiling.

"Charles? Are you in there?" I duck into the bathroom, covering my mouth and nose with my shirt, pulling back the moldy plastic shower curtain. I find the marionettes in the bathtub, flames charring and melting their faces, their bodies crinkled and unrecognizable as Julie or Jess or Charles. I grab a sooty glass cup from beside the sink and fill it again and again, scooping brown, rusty water over the marionettes until the fire smolders, the smoke mixing with steam. The marionettes are no longer recognizable.

I step out into the hallway. My chest feels like it's collapsing. I hear a faint moan from above. There's a fraying string hanging down in front of me and I pull hard, a step-ladder unfolding from the ceiling, leading up into the attic.

I'm blinded by the effect, by the enormity of it all. Charles sits cross-legged in the middle of the attic, illuminated by the fluorescent lights above, blood seeping out of his ears and nose, his eyes glazed over, his limbs twitching with convulsions every few seconds. The walls are plastered with photograph clippings from newspapers and magazines, thousands upon thousands, hanging from the rafters, spread across the wooden floor, photographs of women who look like Julie, of little girls who look like Jess, of men who look like Charles. There's one from the *New York Times* of a blond man and a brunette woman meandering across the beach at Coney Island, hand in hand, their pants rolled up to their knees. Another from *Newsweek* of a blond scientist in the lab, his eyes stark against the white of his lab coat. There's one from *Mothering* magazine of a grinning baby girl, her hair only fuzz, her cheeks plump and pink, holding a sign that says, "Happy Birthday, Daddy!"

A web of strings and pushpins crisscrosses the room, connecting the photographs to one another, as if trying to create meaning. The walls are also covered with writing in red Sharpie. Most of these are notes that Charles wrote to himself, questions, speculations. But soon I discover that there's also a narrative, an alternate narrative, an alternate ending that he's written in which Julie never died, in which Charles and Julie and Jess live happily ever after. He believed in those memories, in that idyllic life he created with Julie and Jess. He couldn't deal with his grief so he changed the narrative. And when Steve and others from the outside world threatened to uncover the falsity of his creations—that was when Julie and Jess disappeared.

"Charles? Charles, have you taken anything?" I ask him. Tears trickle down his face, winding through the wrinkles on his cheeks. He crumples into my shoulder.

"Why didn't they ever come back?" he begs. "What did I do wrong? Why did Julie and Jess have to disappear?"

Charles wobbles and sways with the exertion of speaking. I take his shoulders in my hands, meaning to lay him down across the floor, to let him rest. But instead, my fingers creep closer and he gives a guttural squawk as my fingers wrap around his throat. He looks up at me as his breathing slows, and his eyes are like the universe. The dawn of time. When his breathing stops, I can't let go. I don't know if I'll ever be able to let go.

~

THAT NIGHT, I DREAM ABOUT CHARLES AND JULIE ONE last time. It's a brilliant summer day, blazing asphalt, blasting music, the smell of salt in the air. Charles and Julie can't stop grinning, the wind blowing in their hair. Julie drives. Normally it's Charles but today it's Julie, her cheeks pink, sunburned from the beach. Her brown hair flies in her face, beautiful, long silky hair. Charles sits in the passenger seat, his hair wet and messy from the ocean, a pair of sunglasses propped on his nose. He's drumming away on the dashboard as Julie sings along to the radio, softly at first and then as loud as she can. Her voice is like lavender. Like rain. It's a voice that I will never be able to get out of my head.

Jess sits in the backseat, wrapped in a towel and drinking strawberry lemonade. Her lips are lined with salt and sand and sugar from the lemonade until she licks away the very last of it. And they are finally happy. They are so happy together as they fade away into the melting sunset. This is all they ever needed. This is all they ever wanted.

Acknowledgments

Many thanks to Brian Evenson for his unending support and constant graciousness, and to Thalia Field, Erik Ehn, Marcus Gardley, Renee Gladman, and all of my other brilliant writing professors at Brown University. To Michael Martone, Wendy Rawlings, Kellie Wells, and the rest of the faculty at the University of Alabama for their kindness and their generous feedback. Of course, to my sister, Stephanie Meyers, for reading nearly everything I have ever written. You are the best. And to my father, Ken Meyers, for never trying to make me go to law school. To Ivy Pochoda and Meredith Bailey, thanks for your excellent editorial skills, and to the dream team both currently and formerly at PEN Center USA—Libby Flores, Lilliam Rivera, Michelle Franke, Amanda Fletcher, and all the others. Thank you to everyone who has helped to make this novel happen. Thank you for believing in me—I believe in you too.

About the Author

photo credit: Stephanie Meyers

MICHELLE MEYERS is a fiction writer and playwright born and raised in Los Angeles. Her writing has been published in the *Los Angeles Times*, *Juked*, *Grey Sparrow Journal*, *decomP*, and *jmww,* among others, and her plays have been developed and/or produced all across the United States. She was a 2015 PEN Center Emerging Voices Fellow in Fiction and received her bachelor's degree in Literary Arts and Writing for Performance at Brown University. Meyers is currently an MFA candidate in Fiction at the University of Alabama's Creative Writing program.

SELECTED TITLES FROM SHE WRITES PRESS

She Writes Press is an independent publishing company founded to serve women writers everywhere. Visit us at www.shewritespress.com.

Murder Under The Bridge: A Palestine Mystery by Kate Raphael. $16.95, 978-1-63152-960-3. Rania, a Palestinian police detective with a young son, meets cheeky Jewish-American feminist Chloe at an Israeli checkpoint—and soon becomes embroiled in a murder case that implicates the highest echelons of the Israeli military.

Clear Lake by Nan Fink Gefen. $16.95, 978-1-938314-40-7. When psychotherapist Rebecca Lev's father dies under suspicious circumstances, she becomes obsessed with discovering what happened to him.

Water On the Moon by Jean P. Moore. $16.95, 978-1-938314-61-2. When her home is destroyed in a freak accident, Lidia Raven, a divorced mother of two, is plunged into a mystery that involves her entire family.

In the Shadow of Lies: A Mystery Novel by M. A. Adler. $16.95, 978-1-938314-82-7. As World War II comes to a close, homicide detective Oliver Wright returns home—only to find himself caught up in the investigation of a complicated murder case rife with racial tensions.

Just the Facts by Ellen Sherman. $16.95, 978-1-63152-993-1. The seventies come alive in this poignant and humorous story of a fearful rookie reporter at a small-town newspaper who uncovers a big-time scandal.

Watchdogs by Patricia Watts. $16.95, 978-1-938314-34-6. When journalist Julia Wilkes returns to the town where her career got its start, she is forced to face some old ghosts—and some new enemies.